For beautiful Isla, already a bibliophile.

And a great big thank you to Mitch and Joan.

I0621510

Once Upon a Somewhere

a

Somewhere

A Collection of

Short Stories
by

M.K.Aston

Rycroft Press

First published electronically 2014

This edition published 2015 by Ryecroft Press

ISBN 978-0-9933305-1-3

Contents

Suffering Saffron 1

Mélange à Trois.................................... 13

William the Conqueror....................................... 27

Journey Through Hell................................. 31

Blast From the Past.. 79

That Extra Mile................................... 85

Resisting a Rest..103

London's Alive! 117

Living Without Wings 137

Absurd Assignation...159

Beast of Burden 175

At the End of the Day.......................................185

Suffering Saffron

It was another beautiful late September evening and all across the village blackbirds embroidered the air with their sweet melody, passing their message of cheer from treetop to chimney. High above, the first few spots of celestial magic twinkled in the east while towards the west, where the stubborn glow of the late summer sun still infused the horizon, several planes cut long, pink wounds in the great amethyst sky.

On Hillside View, the village's small housing estate, children played energetically in a garden and the kicks and bounces of their ball echoed around their little patch of fenced-in green. An electric lawnmower came to rest close by as someone finished a job that would probably need redoing within a week. A heavy dog barked listlessly somewhere and another, somewhere else, responded with more vigour.

In the back garden of number twenty-seven, a barbeque filled the air with the primitive aroma of charring meat. Fat dripped onto the white-hot coals beneath the griddle, fizzing and spluttering a random tune, each greasy note a miniature explosion for the senses. Wisps of blue-grey smoke curled up into a billow and, rising quickly from the heat, flew over the fence and floated gently over the adjoining gardens.

On the patio, two couples sat around a garden table laid for dinner. They were chatting easily, their voices a gentle murmur and yet there was something cool and careful in their smiles. After a few moments, one of them raised their glass over the centre of the table.

'To...' Jeff Chandler searched for the appropriate words, 'fresh starts.'

'Oh yes, well done, hun. Fresh starts. I like that.'

'Fresh starts. Here, here.'

'Lovely. Yes. Fresh starts.'

Their glasses chimed delicately as they came together.

'Cheers. Cheers. Yes, cheers. Cheers,' they said. And they all sipped their wine.

'To be honest,' said Sylvia Browning, leaning forward and taking a peanut from a bowl on the table like a sparrow pecking at a feeder, 'when you invited us, we didn't know what to think.' Like the bird, Sylvia was petite and timid. She spoke timidly too and often began a sentence with an apology. Her fashion sense was Oxfam, she never wore make-up and her hair was cut like a boy's.

'Really?' replied Alison Chandler, smiling while surreptitiously studying the other woman's appearance. Alison was more owl in size than sparrow and not at all timid. She lacked the wisdom of the owl but she had an outgoing personality and enjoyed a wide circle of friends. Unlike her neighbour who never considered make-up, Alison never went anywhere without having at least a shimmer of pale blue around her eyes.

'Come on, hun. With our history?' mused Jeff, as though his wife had missed the point entirely. 'What would you've thought if they'd invited us round?' Jeff was a bear of a man, tall but narrow shouldered and wide in the middle. In profile or head on, it didn't matter which, he had the silhouette of a bowling pin.

He was a successful beer drinker, an avid Arsenal supporter but an even more avid gardener. And he was the instigator of this little soirée.

Alison lifted her flat brow and nodded her accord. 'Hmm, I suppose.'

'You joke about that, Jeffrey,' said Jack Browning, his tone a relaxed grumble, like a TVR on tick over, 'but there were a number of times we did think about inviting you.' Jack was sitting one leg crossed over the other and as upright as a bookend. A slim cigar smouldered between two hairy fingers of his left hand. He was the disgruntled citizen of the group, the oldest and most likely the one with the highest blood pressure. He was wire-haired and red faced and often angry at something trivial. With trophy handle ears and close-set eyes, his resemblance to a baboon was not hard to perceive.

'Really?' said Alison, in exactly the same tone of enthralment as before.

'Uh huh, but I don't think Sylvia knew quite how to ask you, did you dear?'

'Sorry dear. No, that's not exactly the reason we didn't invite them,' said Sylvia, still holding on to that peanut. 'Jack always said that…'

'The fact is,' cut in Jack, with an unreadable glance at this wife, 'we're here now and we all want to make this work. Bury the hatchet. Right?'

'Here, here, Jack,' said Jeff. 'We've let a damn silly thing get in the way of a simple neighbourly friendship and I for one am glad we're here now.' He raised his glass in another toast. 'To our neighbours.'

The other three echoed the sentiment and everyone took another sip of wine.

'Hun, how're the kebabs doing?' asked Alison. 'I'm starving.'

'I don't know. Let me ask them.' Jeff heaved himself out of his chair and crossed to the grill. 'Hey kebabs! How're you doing?' He turned back to Alison and shrugged and she groaned at his humour.

'Now,' she began, addressing her guests. 'You told us you don't eat red meat.'

'That's right,' growled Jack, as though any one who did was stupid.

'And we don't like garlic,' added Sylvia quickly. She wrinkled her nose apologetically.

'And you don't like garlic,' repeated Alison. 'Yes, so Jeff, being the ace butcher he is, has come up with something a bit fancy for us all. Haven't you, hun?'

'Oh lovely,' said Sylvia, finally popping that peanut into her mouth.

Jeff put down the tongs and resumed his seat.

'Yes, I've made us all something a little special this evening, it being a special evening and all. I'm not going to tell you what it is yet but for a hint, I'll say - think about the countryside.'

'Oh, sounds intriguing,' said Sylvia, grinning.

'You shouldn't have gone to so much bother for us,' rumbled Jack, as he blew a plume of fragrant smoke above his head.

'Oh, trust me,' said Jeff. 'It's a pleasure. This whole evening is a pleasure.' He raised his glass and drained it. 'How're we all doing for drinks?'

Alison glanced around the table. 'We're all nearly empty. I'll go and get the bottle. Are you both okay with wine or would you like something else?'

'You prefer a beer, Jack?' asked Jeff. 'I've got some nice Belgian stuff indoors. Pretty potent mind. Or there's some run of the mill Heineken or Tetley's. Take your pick.'

Jack pondered for all of three seconds.

'I'll try some of the Belgian if I may. And Sylvia will be okay with the wine. But then, she'll drink anything if you put a straw in it.' He laughed for the first time that evening.

'Sorry, but it helps me cope,' said Sylvia, rolling her eyes and smiling wearily.

Alison laughed.

'There you go, hun,' said Jeff to Alison, who was hovering for the order. 'A bottle of Duvel for me and Jack and put a straw in the wine bottle for Sylvia here.'

A rather affected ripple of laughter went round the table.

'Now then, I hope you're hungry. It should be ready in another minute or two,' said Jeff, getting up again.

'It smells good, I'll say that,' admitted Jack.

'Nothing like the smell of a barbeque to get the juices flowing, is there,' agreed Jeff.

'I'm starving,' said Sylvia, as she took another peanut. 'We usually eat much earlier than this.'

'Don't eat them all,' whispered Jack, with a frown of disapproval. 'You'll fill yourself up.'

'It's only my second one,' countered Alison, in a similar whisper.

'Yes, so do we usually,' said Jeff. 'But sometimes it's nice to sit and have a few drinks first. Let the appetite really swell.'

'Especially on an evening such as this,' said Jack, with a glance up at the cool, clear sky.

'Here we are,' said Alison, re-emerging from the house with a tray of drinks.

'Oh lovely. Thank you.' Alison took her wine - a glass, not the bottle with a straw.

'Marvellous.' Jack accepted the beer and a glass to pour it into. Alison took the other beer to Jeff, who immediately sipped straight from the bottle.

'So, Alison,' said Sylvia, 'I just love the way your garden looks. It's so beautiful. The colours are amazing. How do you get it looking so lovely?'

'Oh, that's Jeff's department. Ask him how he does it. I don't even know the difference between a plant and a flower. I just cut the grass and pull a few weeds, that's about my limit.'

They all glanced around the well-tended garden. The greens looked smoky blue in the fading light.

'Hun, you want to switch the outside light on?' suggested Jeff, pointing with the tongs.

Alison got up and reached an arm inside the kitchen door. A halogen bulb above the patio doors came on and threw a thin wash of brilliance across the garden.

'I must say, your Busy Lizzies are quite something, Jeffrey. I've never had much luck with them myself,' said Jack.

'I'll be honest. They're not from seed. I bought them pretty much as you see them a couple of days ago, which is a first for me. I haven't had much luck with growing things from seed for a while thanks to...'

'Jeff!' broke in Alison sharply, her face momentarily stern. 'How much longer hun?' Her eyes sent a warning.

'A minute or two,' he replied, clearly understanding what she wasn't saying. 'But you know what they say,' he said, continuing his thread with Jack, 'there's a first time for everything. I'll just have to see if they settle.'

'Let's hope so,' said Alison, with a roll of her eyes. 'They cost enough.'

Jeff ignored the comment. 'But I'd say they're probably my favourite perennial. Azaleas too. They give so much colour. I mean, look at them.'

'Yes. And is that a little pear tree in the corner?' observed Jack.

'Actually it's peach, believe it or not.'

'Really? Anything off it?'

'Oh, lovely. I think peaches are my favourite fruit,' admitted Sylvia.

'Three last year but it's looking like only one this year. But that's the way it goes.'

'Oh, not me,' said Alison to Sylvia. 'I like berries. Strawberries. Raspberries.'

'Blackberries!' said Sylvia.

'Oh yes, blackberries,' agreed Alison.

'Well you've certainly put a lot of work into this garden. Makes mine look quite dull.'

'We should go picking one day,' said Alison.

'One day soon,' said Sylvia. 'I know where there are hedgerows loaded with them.'

'Well, I guess it's my thing,' said Jeff, remaining by the grill. 'I spend all day handling carcasses, chopping up meat and bone and the like; I suppose it's the antithesis of my work. Everything out here is alive. It's a challenge too getting things to thrive. Of course, it's even more of one when a certain little someone,' Jeff's tone hardened, 'keeps coming over the fence and digging things up and leaving me disgusting little presents.'

'Jeff! Let's not go there,' said Alison, firmly.

'Sorry, hun,' said Jeff, his voice immediately contrite. 'I did promise didn't I?'

There was a pause during which the sizzling from the barbeque was the only sound. Jeff turned the kebabs. Alison smiled at Sylvia and downed her drink. Sylvia smiled at Alison and tapped her fingers silently on the table and Jack took a firm pull on his cigar.

'It's not as though we instruct her to come over here,' grumbled Jack, with blameless vigour. 'She goes where she wants.'

'Honestly, Jack,' said Alison, 'you don't need to explain.'

'I don't know. Maybe I do. I mean, this is what started the whole bloody business betwee…'

'Sorry Jack, dear.' His wife raised her voice in an uncharacteristic plea. 'Please. Don't.'

'Hun, can you bring the plates over?' Jeff sounded business-like.

Alison gathered the plates and took them to her husband.

'Please let's not argue,' urged Sylvia. 'Let's not waste this lovely evening.'

'Well said, Sylvia,' said Alison, returning to the table and giving the other woman's hand a friendly pat.

A few minutes later, everyone had a pair of kebabs on their plate. Each skewer had four golf balls of meat on them separated by pieces of blackened onion and bell pepper.

'Please help yourselves to everything else,' said Alison. 'It's all garlic-free.' She smiled at Sylvia and the smile was returned.

'Yes. Come on, Jack. Tuck in,' said Jeff. 'Anything else you need?'

'No, I think I'm fine with what's here,' his reply as cool as the spoonful of potato salad he put on his plate. 'How about you, dear?'

'I'm fine,' said Sylvia, as she put a timid amount of coleslaw on the side of her plate. 'This really looks lovely,' she added.

'Everything's lovely when you're really hungry though, isn't it?' said Jeff, a smile easing onto his face and staying there.

The table fell silent again as the four were momentarily occupied in reaching for things to add to their plates.

'So Jeffrey, I notice the meat on my skewers is rather darker than yours.' Jack took a fork and used it to slide the meat and vegetables from the skewer onto his plate. Sylvia cut a piece with her knife and put it in her mouth. 'You sure it's not red meat?' he asked. Sylvia stopped chewing, waiting for Jeff's reply.

'Definitely. It's just that because you two don't like garlic, I compensated by adding a little extra soy sauce and a few extra herbs and the like. That's why yours are darker. But basically, we've all got the same. Pheasant and rabbit minced and made into balls.'

Sylvia resumed chewing. 'Well, it's very nice,' she said between chews. 'An intriguing blend of meats.'

'Different, I'll say that,' said Jack, filling his mouth.

Once again the table fell silent as everyone tucked in, eager to relieve their hunger. Jeff appeared somewhat smug that his meatballs were rapidly disappearing but perhaps understandably; he'd put a lot of work into them.

The women drove the conversation throughout the meal and it never strayed far from being light and rather bland. The men listened but rarely added anything to it. It was clear to all of them that this neighbourly friendship needed some work but at least that all-important first step had been taken.

When the meal was over and the wine and beer glasses were empty, Jeff debuted a rather expensive cognac he'd been saving for an occasion. They all took a little and with the rising alcohol levels the men shared mildly embarrassing anecdotes while the women put what few leftovers there were in the fridge.

'Sorry about that earlier business,' said Sylvia, keeping her voice low to stop it travelling outside.

'Think nothing of it,' replied Alison. 'If it was just you and me, there'd be no problem would there?'

'Trust the men to cause problems.'

'Don't they always,' said Alison, with a laugh.

'It's their speciality.' Sylvia laughed as well. 'Can I help with the dishes?'

'Not at all. I'll get Jeff to help me do all that later. Let's go and finish our drinks.'

'I wouldn't be at all surprised if the problem's over anyway,' said Sylvia, her voice taking on a mournful note as they stepped back outside.

'Oh. Why's that?'

'We haven't seen Saffron for over a week now, have we dear?' Both women resumed their seats. The men stopped their conversation.

'Haven't you?' enquired Alison, sipping her drink.

'She's been gone before,' grumbled Jack. 'My little lady will be back.' He seemed quite certain of the fact.

'For a day or two but never this long,' countered Sylvia. 'Sorry, but I think she's been run over.'

'Don't say such a thing, woman,' growled Jack, throwing back his brandy. 'How could you? Nothing of the sort has happened.'

'You hear that, hun?'

Jeff was lost for a moment in his garden, smiling serenely at his colourful borders.

'Hun?'

'Sorry what?'

'Their cat. It hasn't come home for almost a week.'

'Ah. Well, I'm sure it's not far away.'

'Sylvia thinks it might have been run over.' Alison's tone was sympathetic but her eyes flickered with just the faintest hint of hope that it might be true.

'Saffron has not been run over,' stated Jack, with vigour. However, the possibility was clearly in his mind because he suddenly became fidgety and uncomfortable. He glanced at his watch and signalled to his wife that it was probably time they were going.

'I'm with you Jack,' said Jeff, his face wearing the comfortable grin of a satisfied man. 'I reckon she's around here somewhere.'

Jack grunted in appreciation of the support. But he made his excuses and rose to leave. Sylvia apologised for not finishing her brandy and rose as well. After a short medley of 'thanks' and 'lovely meal' and 'we must do this again soon', the Chandlers closed their front door and their neighbours went home.

Jeff and Alison returned to the garden and continued clearing the table.

'I think that went well for the most part,' said Alison, with less conviction than she'd have liked.

'The kebabs were excellent. You did well there. But you men! My God, you make it so difficult.'

'It did go well,' agreed Jeff. 'And I'm so happy they liked their food. A little surprised but very happy. Very happy indeed.' He seemed to be talking to himself and he ignored his wife's final comment altogether. The table was soon cleared but the washing up was a jumbled stack in the sink. Alison became thoughtful as she shook the crumbs from the tablecloth. Her brow suddenly took on a look of worry.

'Funny that the cat should go missing just before you go and spend a load on the garden,' whispered Alison, as she followed Jeff inside. She knew her husband well enough to know that he would never waste money.

'Hmm. A coincidence.'

'Jeff?' There was suspicion in her tone as her face became stern.

'What?'

The back door closed and the patio light went out. Next door, a light came on and the back door opened. Jack Browning stepped outside and his shadow remained close to his feet as he called out - 'Saffron! Saffron. Here kitty, kitty, kitty!'

Mélange à Trois

The early May sun was high and bright and the high street crawled with the lunchtime crowd. Office workers, happy for the respite from their air-conditioned yokes emerged from the buildings like ants through gaps in the pavement. This way and that they went in their shirts and ties, blouses and skirts, into shops and delis to pluck sandwiches from fridges or to stand in lines and wait while agile fingers wearing disposable gloves made them something to order. The office workers shared the queues with their overall-wearing brothers as well as the kids from the local comprehensive; everyone dressed more or less in their appropriate uniform.

The weather encouraged the people to remain outside and many of them sat and smiled freely on the benches that dotted the pavements or any other place that offered a suitable perch. The little square of green down by the river behind the town's main car park offered a haven of tranquillity filled with daisies and cherry blossom, butterflies and birdsong and many people enjoyed taking their break there. Some sat in gregarious groups that would occasionally interrupt the tranquillity with bursts of unabashed laughter; others sat quietly in pairs, their conversations just a gentle murmur and some sat by themselves not speaking at all, unhurried-looking individuals perfectly content to be absorbed in a newspaper or a novel. They sat on the grass and on the benches or simply wandered slowly around the path eating and observing, grateful just to be outside in the fresh, warm air.

The modern styling of the council offices led the majority of locals to label it the ugliest building in town and with its uncomfortable fusion of Cubism and Deconstructivism it was easy to sympathise. The architect leading the design team had had a field day with his imagination and with its unlikely angles, chocolate coloured brickwork and smoked glass windows it appeared like a giant stack of half-melted brownies at the end of the small business park. In its planning stages, such had been the opposition to its construction that a petition had circulated and garnered close to three thousand signatures, the list including a number of prominent individuals within the community. But not unusually, there are times, particularly within the political world, when the ears of reason are deliberately plugged and the scales of justice unfairly balanced so that things come to pass regardless of the wishes of the taxpayer. The only saving grace for the locals was that a gentle curve in the little cul-de-sac hid the building from an otherwise photogenic high street and so the monstrosity didn't offend appreciators of fine Victorian architecture unless they deliberately sought it out.

Lee Dedham was at his desk on the third floor of the monstrosity winding up a call on his phone. As he spoke, his voice merged with the gentle murmur of the open plan setting.

'And that's a hundred and sixty, right? Nice one. Okay, see you soon. Thanks. Thanks a lot.'

The call ended and he dropped his mobile into the breast pocket of his shirt. He leaned back in his chair and stretched, enjoying the broad grin that spread across his turnip-shaped face. He then reached for the grey phone on his desk and dialled an extension.

'Hi. You ready to go?' he said, when his call was answered. 'Nice one. Right, I'll see you downstairs. Just remember though, I gotta go and…okay, just testing. Yeah okay, see you in a bit.' His voice was pitched higher than his size would suggest and the words flowed a little too rapidly into sentences often making him difficult to understand. There would be the briefest of pauses for a thought or a breath and then he'd go again, rattling out the words the way a machine gun spits bullets only to come to another abrupt stop. To hear him speak was reminiscent of a woodpecker doing its thing against a tree trunk. Not quite but almost.

He signalled to his supervisor, who was sitting across from him, that he was off to lunch and with a nod he headed swiftly for the lift with heavy steps.

Two minutes later he emerged through the main doors of the building into the sunlight. Beside him walked Carol Rush, a receptionist on the main desk who also happened to be one of his wife's best friends. She was middle-aged and pleasant in every aspect and appeared quite petite alongside Lee's oafish bearing.

'I'm looking forward to seeing this picture you've had made for her. It sounds intriguing. What's the word for it again?' Her voice matched her appearance and her dress sense. It was precise, uncluttered.

'Len - tic - u - lar,' said Lee, emphasising each syllable in a moment of unrushed speech. He pulled out his wallet and a fat thumb counted the notes tucked inside. 'I'm looking forward to seeing it too. Should be good for what it's costing. It's cleared me out. You look at it from one angle and it's of us when we were dating, you step sideways and it morphs into us as we are now. It's like stepping through twenty years. Here you go.'

He handed Carol a fiver.

'Oh. You want your usual?'

'Only if you're going to Luigi's.'

'Where else would I be going?'

'Nice one. Then I'll have corned beef and pickle on white, thanks. No salad.'

'Ugh! You wouldn't eat that stuff if you knew what was actually in it.'

'Maybe not, but I'd rather not know,' said Lee, an amused pig-like snort rounding off the admission.

'I love the idea of the picture though and I think Kim will be thrilled with it. And she knows nothing about it?'

'The whole day's going to be one big surprise. She thinks I forgot.'

'You mean like you usually do?'

'Yeah,' admitted Lee, his tone sagging with shame.

'You know, I really should apologise to her for the other day,' said Carol.

'Why's that then?'

'Well, I was in the middle of something when she called round and I think I may have been a bit rude. She didn't say anything to you about it, did she?'

Lee glanced at Carol and smiled.

'One reason I survived these twenty years of marriage,' he said, 'is because I pay very little attention to what you women get up to. If you two have an issue, it's none of my business. You'll sort it out, I'm sure.'

'Yes, I know. But we've been a bit distant these last few months, as I'm sure you know but would rather not, and I don't understand why. I don't know what's changed.'

'All I ask is you don't ruin the party tomorrow night. I want everything to be perfect.'

'Oh God, no. I'd never do that. You know me better than that, surely?'

'I know you women are crazy, I know that. How I managed to stay married to one for two decades is a mystery!'

'Ah. Yes you do. You two are made for each other and you know it.'

'Just as well, isn't it, 'cos I doubt no one else would have us,' said Lee, snorting with amusement again.

They turned into an alleyway that led through to the high street and their shadows were small at their feet.

'There'll be a queue at Luigi's, always is on a day like this,' said Lee, 'so I might get done before you've been served. I'll come and look for you, anyway.'

'Let's go to the park instead of back to the office. It's such a lovely day,' said Carol.

'Good idea.'

They turned into the busy little high street and straightaway saw several people standing outside the glass fronted Luigi's. It may have been the smallest delicatessen in town but it had a reputation of quality and while it wasn't the cheapest, those who went there were of the mind that a good sandwich was worth paying for.

'Well,' said Carol, 'looks like I'm standing in a queue for the next ten minutes.'

'It's not as long as it could be,' observed Lee. 'I'll be as quick as I can. I'm just in the arcade but if you get done before I'm back, wait for me and we'll head to the park together.'

'Okay,' said Carol, as she pushed the button at the crossing even though it had already been pushed. Lee continued along the high street, his ungainly march marking him out as a man on a mission.

By the time he turned into the arcade midway along the high street, Carol was standing in the queue outside Luigi's. Between the open door and the counter inside, five customers were standing shoulder to shoulder either waiting for their orders or waiting to be served. This meant that the next in line had to wait until someone came out before they could go in. It was a given that if you wanted a Luigi's at lunchtime, you'd probably have to queue outside even in nasty weather and once you were inside, you'd be squeezed like a pilchard in a can.

The air in the arcade was cool and the art nouveau style floor tiles echoed Lee's footsteps as he passed the designer boutiques and overpriced cafés on his way to the art emporium.

Across the road from the arcade was the trendy, read-a-pile-of-magazines-while-you-wait hair salon, Flossy's. Standing at the reception counter inside with her purse in her hand and her hair in a neatly cut bob was Kim Dedham.

'I can't tell you how grateful I am that you were able to fit me in at such short notice,' she said, with a smile that relayed relief as well as joy.

'Oh, no problem, Mrs Dedham,' said the young and heavily made up stylist. 'You called just after we had a cancellation. We were happy to do it.' Kim paid electronically and as she turned her attention to the diary to book her next appointment, she happened to glance out the window to catch her husband turn into the arcade across the road. Her cheerful expression lengthened in surprise. A few minutes later she stepped out onto the pavement and pulled out her mobile phone.

Lee was smiling as he regarded the picture. He held its narrow rosewood frame and tilted it this way and that, changing the image from one picture to the other. The two photographs he had selected had come out well; they were sharp and their colour was vibrant. He was certain that Kim would love it and that it would take pride of place on the sitting room wall.

'Have you got something I can carry it in?' asked Lee.

'Certainly, sir,' said the bow tie wearing proprietor, whose head was tilted as he listened intently to his customer's scurrying speech. He reached beneath the counter and pulled out a white paper bag the size of a fridge door. The shop's name was printed in curling red script on both sides. The man, who was thin and softly spoken, quickly enveloped the picture in bubble wrap, expertly folding and taping the edges before slipping it into the bag.

'Nice one,' said Lee, handing across the required amount of cash. 'Thanks a lot'.

'Thank you,' said the proprietor, counting the notes and then stowing them in the till. 'I hope your wife likes it.'

'Yeah, I hope so too,' said Lee, moving towards the door just as his phone rang in his breast pocket.

'Oh, and congratulations on your anniversary,' said the proprietor, with a final smile.

'Thanks,' said Lee, reaching for his phone. It was Kim. He stepped outside before answering it.

'Hiya,' he said, as he retraced his steps to meet Carol at Luigi's. 'What's up?' He listened for a moment and his face grew tense. He stopped walking. 'Why, where are you?' His tone became direct, his eyes shifty, and as he listened he considered the large bag in his hand. Then his eyes widened and his bottom lip became a target for his teeth. 'The arcade? No reason. I just wanted to have a look around. Where are you then?' he asked again, as a forced smile looked more like a sneer on his face. He looked towards the high street and then turned around and began hurrying towards the rear of the arcade where it led to the car park. 'Oh, nice one!' he said. His voice sounded a little unsteady as he trotted along in a most ungraceful fashion, like John Cleese with a dog snapping at his heels. 'Yeah, sure we can. Just give me a minute and I'll come out and meet you. No, no. You stay where you are; I'll come to you. Yeah, just give me a minute.' He ended the call and immediately made another.

Carol had one foot inside Luigi's. The aroma of freshly ground coffee beans wafted past her. Three men with Mediterranean looks toiled behind the counter, taking and making orders. A radio played a mix of music and chat somewhere behind them. The fingers of the men moved swiftly, two of them selecting ingredients from deep white dishes behind the glass display and creating sandwiches and baguettes of distinction, cutting them across the middle, wrapping them in greaseproof paper and securing them with an elastic band. The third man worked the Sanremo espresso machine as though it were an extension of his body. He also fed the money into the till. All three displayed a dexterity that was engaging to watch. There was very little chat between them during these busy times.

Carol's phone rang in her handbag. She reached for it and took the call.

'Lee! Are you...? No, not yet but I'm next. Why? What? No, I'm here now.'

A man in a navy suit that was desperately in need of pressing squeezed his way past her, his lunch held against his chest like a winning hand of cards.

'Next!' called one of the sandwich makers.

'Oh Lee, that's me. They're calling me in,' said Carol into the phone. She eased herself into the little shop. 'Yes, but...no. But Lee...' Her pleasant face suddenly took on a scowl and lost a little of its pleasantness. 'Oh, fine. But I'm not queuing again. Oh, whatever. I'll see you there.' She expelled a lungful of frustration and pushed her way brusquely back out into the sunshine.

She made it to the car park in less than two minutes using an access road off the high street. Lee appeared from behind a parked van and came towards her carrying the large bag. He moved quickly with an eye over his shoulder.

'Sorry about this, Carol,' he said, with feeling, 'but if she sees the bag the surprise will be ruined. I had no idea she was in town.'

'It's okay,' said Carol. 'I understand.' The annoyance she had shown when leaving Luigi's had already evaporated like spilt water on a hot flagstone. 'Tomorrow night must be perfect. Besides, it was only a sandwich. I'll go to Sainsbury's instead. I'm certainly not joining that queue again. Here, let me take it. I'll see you back at the office in a while.'

'Thanks Carol. I owe you one.'

'All right if I take a peek?'

'You can't,' he replied, as he turned to go. 'The bloke wrapped it. But I'll show you when I get back to the office, if you like. See you.'

Carol mouthed 'see you,' and watched him disappear into the arcade. Then she turned towards the bustling supermarket.

Kim was looking at a window display in a clothing boutique when Lee finally got to her. Her eyes were devouring a ridiculously expensive pair of diamond-studded sandals. A few doors further and she would have been at the art emporium. Lee's relief was all over his face as he sidled up to her.

'Fancy running into you here,' he said, cheerily.

Kim turned away from the window.

'Oh, there you are. What kept you? And why the cheesy grin?'

Lee reigned in his relief and his expression softened.

'No reason. Just happy to see you, I guess.'

The corner of Kim's mouth curled in doubt.

'Nice haircut,' added Lee.

'You like it?'

'Yes, I do.'

'Are you alright?' Kim looked at her husband suspiciously.

'Yes, why?'

'I don't know,' she said, carefully. 'You seem a bit…smug.'

'Smug? Well, I dunno about that. No, I just bumped into Carol and she said something that made me laugh, maybe that's it. That's why I was a couple of minutes. Now, do you want something to eat?'

'Yes, I want a Luigi's.'

'Okay, let's go then. There's bound to be a queue though.'

They walked out of the arcade side by side and into the sunny high street.

'And how is Carol?' asked Kim, as they walked along. She sounded a little disgruntled.

'Don't you know? I thought you two were best pals.'

'So did I. But she's been off with me recently and I don't know why. She's been acting cold towards me. She hasn't said anything to you?'

'Nope.' Lee gave a non-committal shrug. 'You women are crazy.'

When they reached Luigi's, Lee was able to put a foot on the doorstep.

'Nice one,' he said. 'This shouldn't take long. What do you want?'

'Their smoked salmon salad on granary.'

'Trust you to want the most expensive.'

'I can't help it if I've got expensive taste,' said Kim, smiling. Lee rolled his eyes and pulled out his wallet but stopped before opening it.

'Oh. This is embarrassing,' he said. He dug into his trouser pockets and pulled out a few coins.

'What is?'

'I've come out without any money.'

'You're joking? How were you going to pay for your lunch?'

'I dunno. I guess I forgot to go to the cash point. I'll go now. Mine's corn beef and pickle on white if you get served before I'm back.'

'No, you stay here,' said Kim. 'I'll go. I need some cash anyway. I'll be as quick as I can.'

'Well, don't you have enough on you to pay?'

'No, I'm out. Won't be long.'

Kim separated from the line and moved off down the pavement to find an ATM. Lee watched her go and then stepped into the shop after a hungry looking woman came out carrying her freshly made lunch.

Kim continued on past the nearest cash machine. There was a queue of precious minutes for it and it wouldn't have printed out the mini statement that she liked to get with her withdrawals. She crossed the road and made her way towards her own bank, which was situated on the corner of the access road to the car park behind Sainsbury's. There were a couple of people queuing to use the machine outside and so she moved on past to try the machine inside. But as she did so, she recognised the petite figure of Carol in the queue. She was the last in line and she was standing serenely with a large white bag in her hand. Kim saw the bag was from the art emporium in the arcade and her brow jumped in admiration. She stopped but then thought better of it and carried on inside. But then she stopped again and turned and took a few steps back.

'Hello, Carol.' Her tone was a little careful, almost as though she was addressing an acquaintance rather than a good friend. Carol had been daydreaming and was caught completely off guard. She flinched as if someone had shouted 'Boo!' in her ear.

'Kim! What are you doing here?' Carol went from relaxed and dreamy to tense and awkward in an instant.

'I could ask you the same thing but it's a bit obvious, isn't it?' Kim smiled and indicated the line Carol was standing in. 'So, how have you been?'

'Fine.' The word shot out cold and blunt like a steel bolt and Carol drew her hands surreptitiously behind her back. Kim noticed the movement.

'Been shopping, I see.'

'No. I mean, yes.' Carol looked uncomfortable, frightened almost. If she'd been wearing a collar she would have fingered it. Her eyes seemed reluctant to meet those of her friend. There was an awkward pause and then Carol suddenly turned and hurried away uttering a desperate apology as she went. Kim watched perplexed as her friend zigzagged away frantically between the other pedestrians on the pavement. She sighed and slowly shook her head as her expression became vacant for a moment but then she caught herself dawdling and stepped up to the now unoccupied cash machine.

As 2 o'clock approached, the high street became perceptibly emptier. Those making their way back to their places of work did so at a leisurely pace. The rushing about to get lunch and to secure a suitable spot to sit out and enjoy it had passed and a lethargy had taken its place, brought about by the need to withdraw from the beautiful sunshine and the prospect of the afternoon's work.

Lee approached the reception desk of the chocolate brownie building with an apology on his face. Carol was directing a call as he approached and when she saw him she frowned. While she was talking she reached down to one side of her chair for Lee's bag but she didn't lift it onto the desk until she'd finished the call.

'You mister, are going to explain to your wife as soon as she's opened this why I behaved so oddly. Okay?' There was no trace of amusement on her face as she handed the bag to Lee.

'I know. Don't worry. I will,' replied Lee, stifling a laugh.

'It's not funny. She must think I'm...' Carol's tone was severe. 'Well, I can't begin to think what she thinks of me.'

'Don't worry,' said Lee, 'I'll explain it to her. Now, do you wanna look?'

'No, thank you. I'll see it tomorrow night.'

'Oh, about that,' said Lee, tiptoeing around a point. 'Kim says she doesn't want you there.'

Carol's eyes lit up and she drew in a deep breath of defiance but before she could get a word of protest out, Lee pulled away from the desk.

'Only joking,' he said, with a wink. 'See you tomorrow.'

William the Conqueror

Against the dark corrugated iron roof its body looked like a small sweet, an orange fruit pastille perhaps and about as thick. Tiny white spots covered its back and its legs, which weren't very long but were thick and looked more like those of a crustacean. Although William had never seen it move, he knew it was very much alive.

Like most children, William was happiest when playing with his friends. It could be football or cricket or some magical fantasy dreamt up from their youthful imaginations, it didn't matter, it was always fun. But he also had his share of weekend chores and truth be told, most of them, he didn't mind. Naturally, they changed with the seasons but whether he was wielding a broom across an autumnal patio, vacuuming the interior of his father's car or working up a sweat with the old push-mower, it gave him a sense of purpose and pride to be outdoors helping his father.

However, the mention of one particular task and his cheeks would drain of colour and he'd suddenly lose all enthusiasm for being helpful for it would place him in the realm of the spider.

Tidy the garden shed.

The shed sat beneath the over-reaching branches of his neighbour's huge apple tree at a point where the patio ended and the lawn began. His father had built it some years before to his own specification and had incorporated a sturdy workbench at one end plus an abundance of strategically placed nails and hooks around the upper framework to hold every kind of tool from the smallest screwdriver to the largest pickaxe. Old jam jars filled with nuts, screws, washers and other such minutiae hung from the cross members – their lids nailed into the beams and the jars screwed up into them. The shed was home to the mower, the wheelbarrow, a pair of sun beds and a paddling pool plus many other items of garden paraphernalia. It was also where William kept his bicycle.

To be tasked with spring-cleaning this musty grotto of cobwebs and dark corners was his biggest fear and William would employ every excuse and delaying tactic in his young arsenal to avoid doing it. Unfortunately, his father was equally persistent and so despite William's protests, he would eventually have to steel himself and enter the fray.

William was not sure where his loathing of spiders had come from - he'd never been bitten by one or awoken to see one crawling across his pillow - but he could not recall ever feeling comfortable around them, despite his parents' assurances that, they are far more afraid of you than you are of them. He simply could not function normally in close proximity to anything larger than a money spider.

And in the ominous confines of the shed, where the air was damp and scented with sawdust, mildew and creosote, moving things that hadn't been touched for months scared the life out of him.

He gave himself a buffer zone of sorts and a faint sense of being less exposed to the immediate action by using a rake as an arm extension to drag things from their resting places. Anything that was buried behind a layer of soft, grey webbing was given a good tug after which he would run out of the shed for a few minutes to allow any disturbed spiders to disappear out of sight again.

More often than not, he wouldn't actually see any but the yards of dense woven silk hanging like miniature hammocks in the corners spoke volumes. And when he did see one, its frantic arachnid scurrying sent him shivering for safety outside.

Every now and again, particularly when autumn fell, William would encounter a spider in the house, itself a serious enough intrusion of his space but a swiftly deployed shoe would usually put an end to the drama. However, being in the shed was a different thing altogether.

Firstly, he felt like the intruder; the shed being part of the wild outdoors where all of nature's undomesticated critters flourished and roamed free. Secondly, to encounter a spider on a wide flat surface like a floor or a wall gave him a mild sense of control over it but to come upon one in the nooks and crannies of a shed, in amongst a stack of old shelving or caught up beneath a pile of dustsheets where the spider could scuttle away back out of sight was entirely different.

But eventually after a week or two of half-hearted stints when even the flimsiest of excuses would happily end his session's progress, the shed would be cobweb-free and everything would have been swept down and rearranged neatly or replaced in its proper space.

The orange spider in the roof however, remained untouched. It looked so different from any other spider he had ever seen that he was doubly fearful of it. He had no idea how fast it moved or whether his parents' verbal assurance applied; perhaps it wasn't afraid of him at all and would happily defend itself with a venomous efficiency if provoked.

As he worked, William was constantly aware of his proximity to it - indeed a sort of cylindrical exclusion zone was set up around it, a floor to ceiling force field that his body simply could not penetrate.

To inform his father that the job was finally done and ready for his inspection filled William with the kind of relief matched only by the dentist informing him after a good poke around that his teeth were fine and that he'd see him again in six months. His relief was boosted further when his father later informed him that he had removed the orange fruit pastille from the roof that William had bellyached so much about.

Even though the cobwebs and dust would return soon enough, putting his bike away that evening in a clean, tidy shed was very satisfying indeed.

Journey Through Hell

15 October 1987 - 4:35 p.m.

Kevin Connelly was in the zone, running on autopilot. His movements were swift yet controlled and his eyes were judging the lines and gaps of the wall he was building to a keen degree of precision. It was a low wall so he was on his knees but the protective rubber pads he had strapped around his work jeans made the position less uncomfortable. He moved like a machine, swivelling his upper body from the waist, right arm extending and retracting like that of a robot in a factory - scoop some mortar from his hawk, plop it on top of the wall, slide it smooth; select a brick, lay it, bed it in with a tap of the trowel handle, swipe off the excess mortar. Scoop, plop, slide…

His plan had been to finish the job by lunchtime but his morning had been abortive. He just hadn't been able to get on and it had put him behind schedule. But even now as his rhythmic movements were striving to put him on course to finish today, rain clouds were rolling in from the southwest threatening to disappoint him.

The mossy lawn cushioned Elaine Carmichael's footsteps as she crossed from the house to where Kevin was working. She was carrying a small plastic tray on which were a cup of tea and some biscuits. The little china cup rattled elegantly in its saucer.

'A spot of overtime today, is it?' enquired Mrs Carmichael, amiably. Her voice didn't match her slender, refined appearance; it was thick and glutinous like hot tar, fashioned by a lifetime of smoking cigarettes.

The intrusion startled Kevin and in turn, his reaction startled Mrs Carmichael. The teacup rattled alarmingly but she recovered quickly.

'I'm so terribly sorry,' she said, with a hand resting against her chest. 'Did I make you jump?'

Kevin put his trowel and hawk down on the mixing board and rose from his kneeling position. He was laughing but it was for relief rather than from delight.

'Jeez, just a bit, Mrs Carmichael. But it was my fault. I was miles away.' He patted his chest and rolled his eyes elaborately as if a serious accident had just been avoided.

'Oh, I'm just awful, aren't I? Next time, I'll whistle on my way over or better yet, I'll hang a cowbell around my neck.'

'Really, Mrs Carmichael, there's no need for that. I was just thinking about something, that's all.'

'Oh, well, here.' She offered the tea tray. 'Perhaps this'll help settle your nerves again. I was just saying to Herb, you're usually packing up and getting ready to go home by now but I saw you were still in the thick of it so I thought you might like another cup of tea.'

'Thanks,' said Kevin, accepting the tray. His hands were smirched with varying shades of drying mortar which looked rather like camouflage paint.

'How's it coming along?' she asked, with a glance at the freshly laid brickwork. 'Looks very smart, I must say.'

'Yeah, it's going okay,' replied Kevin, with less conviction than he'd have liked. He looked around for a place to rest the tray and quickly found that a comparatively clean corner of his mortarboard seemed as good a place as any. He kept hold of the cup though as well as one of the biscuits.

In a few weeks there would be an elegant, custom-built greenhouse sitting on top of the wall he had very nearly finished. He'd laid the foundations earlier in the summer as well as the herringbone patterned brick path that ran the length of the base then returned a few days ago to start on the wall. For a place to grow tomatoes and nurture pot plants Kevin thought it was a bit extravagant but then, the Carmichaels were extravagant people.

'I was hoping to get it done this morning as they reckon on the weather turning nasty any moment,' said Kevin, raising his eyes to the thickening clouds.

'Yes, I've just heard on the radio they're forecasting gale force winds along the coast this evening although whether that includes us here, heaven only knows. Yet at lunchtime, they didn't say anything about gales, just that we're in for a lot more rain.'

'Do you think they really know?'

'Well, they can't, can they? It must be an absolute devil to predict. The best they can do is give us an idea. I tell you, I take my umbrella with me even if they say it'll be fine.'

Kevin laughed as he started on the biscuit.

'The barometer in the hall's been dropping since around noon though and that's a fair indication we're in for a rough time,' added Mrs Carmichael. Then with a glance up at the sky she asked, 'So, do you think you'll get finished today?'

'If the rain holds off, I should be done within the hour,' said Kevin, his tone was as much cynical as it was hopeful as he looked again at the gathering clouds. He then looked down at his work and pointed out what he had left to do. 'Just got to lay these last few bricks then point up. Oh, and while you're here, can I ask - is it okay to leave some of this stuff here 'til Monday?' With a general sweep of his arm he indicated the pile of surplus bricks and other materials that lay on the grass close by. 'Some of my tools I'll take with me but I'll come back for everything else after the weekend, if that's okay.'

'Oh, that's fine. We've put up with a building site out here for almost a year. A few more days won't harm us.'

'It's going to look posh when it's finished though, isn't it?' said Kevin, his mouth working on the remainder of the biscuit. 'I reckon it's as big as the ground floor of my house.'

'Yes, well that's Herbert for you. All I wanted was a nice little greenhouse to clear things out from the conservatory and he has to go off on some wild design fantasy and build something that's far larger than we'll ever need.' She sounded happy about it yet resigned, as though Herbert was a high-spirited child who didn't often do what he was told and yet as long as he wasn't doing any harm, it was easier to let him have his fun.

Kevin laughed before downing his tea and returning the cup to the saucer on the tray. A quick glance at his watch spurred him on. He picked up the tray and passed it back to Mrs Carmichael with thanks, removing another biscuit in the process.

'Well then, I'll leave you to it,' she said, turning to go.

'Thanks. I'll let you know when I'm off.'

'That's fine. Cheerio.'

She moved away across the lawn as discreetly as she had come, the cup and saucer rattling a gentle tune as she went. Kevin put the whole biscuit in his mouth and then bent to his task. He picked up the trowel and with it, massaged the mix that remained on the mortarboard. He added a splash of water from a bucket and massaged it again, chopping and slicing and gliding the tool through the smooth taupe-coloured paste until he was satisfied with it. Then, plopping a heap on his hawk, he selected a brick and continued where he'd left off.

A light wind moved around the garden stirring the leaves on the trees and waving the sprawling conifers lazily among the crowded borders. The rusty weathercock sitting on top of the chimney squeaked as it moved momentarily and then squeaked again as it inched back to where it had been.

So far, October had been a considerably wet month, the sun mostly hidden behind swathes of thick Atlantic cloud but as if it wanted to remind everyone that it was still there it had found a window of opportunity to shine on and off throughout the morning.

Kevin's morning had been far from sunny though. He had hoped to get a good early start at the Carmichaels so that he could have finished and been on his way home shortly after lunch but Jenny's admission at breakfast that she might be pregnant had done to his orderly thoughts what a whirlwind would do to a neatly raked pile of leaves. For the first few hours, he'd found it almost impossible to concentrate on anything else; even getting out of his van had taken an effort to drag his mind from the possibilities that this revelation had engendered.

He'd almost been out of the door, lacing up his boots on the mat when she'd said in that 'Oh, by the way,' manner that she was a month late. Kevin hadn't been sure if he'd heard correctly but then she quickly attempted to placate his fears by adding that sometimes it can happen to a girl; missing a monthly didn't necessarily mean a baby was on its way. Any number of things could interrupt a girl's natural cycle, stress being one of them. And she'd certainly had her fair share of that lately, what with the hospital changing her roster and her father passing away. Jenny had begged him not to worry and said that they would speak about it later when she got home from her shift or, if he wasn't awake, in the morning before he went to work. But for Kevin, she might just as well have told a fish not to swim. How could he possibly not worry?

Having a baby was a massive step - possibly a step too far - and as he'd driven to work that morning in a sort of daze, he couldn't help but feel he was just a little too young at the moment for such a responsibility. He was only just getting over the momentous step they had taken last year when they had decided to move in together. Renting their poky little two up two down that came with mildew and draughts and the constant reassessment of their monthly budget was about as big a bite of reality as he felt he could handle right now. And yet, over the course of the morning, the thought of being a dad began to scare him less and less. The idea that he, Kevin Connelly, had created life, a brand new human being with the woman he adored, was bordering on the miraculous. It was a big step, of course it was, just as it was for anyone else and yet it wasn't an impossible step to make. So the timing wasn't right but was it ever? Yes, the more he considered it, the less it seemed to trouble him.

Kevin shook his head and again tried to shoulder the thoughts aside so that he could concentrate on laying the last few bricks and finishing the wall. The light had started to fade now and so his urgency increased. Scoop, plop, slide; select another brick, bed it in with a tap of the trowel handle, swipe off the excess mortar. Scoop, plop, slide…

Then with one last check of his levels he removed the string line and got on with the pointing.

A short while later, in the descending gloom, he swept the face of the wall with a soft brush then washed his tools in the bucket of water. His relief that he had beaten the rain was well earned and well timed because the first spots of rain arrived like mischievous imps from the clouds, pattering down across the garden intent on disrupting his progress.

Kevin quickly tidied up then threw his tools together in the bucket to take with him. Finally, he covered the newly laid brickwork with an old plastic tarpaulin and anchored it to the ground with leftover bricks. Job done. Home time.

Mrs Carmichael was basting a roast at the oven when he tapped on the kitchen window and waved goodbye. She raised a free hand in response and her mouth mimed a farewell. Kevin pulled open the heavy wrought iron gate, passed down the side of the red brick garage and out onto the gravelled driveway where his vagabond of a Morris van was parked against a bank of flowerless rhododendrons. He wrenched open the rear doors, hefted in his bucket and quickly sat in behind the wheel out of the rain. He rolled a cigarette as the rain became more determined.

It was a six-mile journey from the Carmichaels' beautiful oast house to the little two up two down Kevin rented on the outskirts of Maydown Common with Jenny Dwyer, his girlfriend of three years. They lived at number 7, in a dark brick terrace of eight situated on an unmade track, a little way out of the village. The potholed track continued on between untamed hedgerows for about five hundred yards down to an old pumping station, which gave the terrace its address - Pumphouse Cottages.

A row of plane trees strangled around their bases by an unruly hedgerow separated the track from the neighbouring property and it was along here that the residents parked their cars. Each cottage had their space, unmarked by paint or post but designated by a simple unspoken neighbourly cooperation. Those households with more than one car had to use the verge out on the lane as well, a practice that in some ways was the better option.

Kevin pulled up at an angle opposite his front door, which like the other doors of the cottages had no garden to gaze upon. Instead they all opened onto an L of drab paving slabs upon which everyone kept their dustbins. A couple of the front doors were brightly painted - one red one yellow - which injected the only colour to an otherwise gloomy frontage; the rest were of a dark hue to help disguise the fact that they were usually dirty from the dust of a dry track or the muddy splashes from a wet one.

Kevin pushed open his front door and took off his boots. He flicked a switch and a shaded bulb in the middle of the ceiling illuminated the main room. It was a small but snug room with an eclectic mix of handed-down furniture. A patterned rug covered a threadbare carpet while magnolia painted woodchip covered the walls. A two-seater sofa and a wooden framed armchair were angled towards a TV and video in the front corner while a small sideboard on which sat a mini HiFi system rested against the back wall. There were a thoughtful number of accessories dotted about, picture frames and ornaments and so on although not so much as to clutter, more to suggest a homemaker had indulged a few whimsical fancies.

Kevin crossed the room in his socks and went through to the kitchen, which was a similar size to the front room. A small table with two chairs and a three-tier clothes airer consumed the space along the inner wall while the cooker, sink and worktop filled the area beneath a window that overlooked a long, narrow back garden. The paintwork was bright and the linoleum floor was clean and unmarked.

Kevin washed his hands in the sink and then glanced at Jenny's looping scrawl on the notepad on the table. He then opened the fridge. As had quickly become her habit when she was on the late shift, she prepared dinner before she left for work; all he had to do was to follow the instructions she'd left him. Tonight it was lasagne and according to the note, it had to go in the oven at gas mark 5 for 50 minutes.

Make sure you allow the oven to heat up for about 20 mins, warned the note. While he waited for this to happen, he stood against the sink sipping a can of Fosters, mulling over the same thing he'd been thinking of all day.

The extra financial burden of having a baby quickly became Kevin's greatest fear. As tight as things were now, he realised they would surely get a whole lot tighter. Obviously Jenny would be away from work and they would have only his income to live on, though for how long he couldn't say. Child benefit would offer some help but again how much, he hadn't a clue.

He frowned at the beer can in his hand and wondered if even something so small would become out of reach, a luxury they would no longer be able to afford. He then thought of all the things they wanted, all the things they had verbally added to their long and short term shopping lists. His eyes glazed. They wanted plenty. But for the most part, they were little things, things that could be saved up for, things that would come in the fullness of time. There were bigger things too of course, but those things - the newer cars, the nicer house in the village, the holidays abroad - they were their dreams, the things that they may or may not get depending on how fortune favoured them. They were the same dreams everyone had, the things that pulled the world out of bed on dark miserable mornings and urged it aboard the treadmill of everyday life.

Kevin shook his head and regained his focus. He was getting ahead of himself - Jenny might not even be pregnant. He finished his beer and crushed and tossed the can in the bin. Then, assuming the oven was up to temperature, he put the lasagne in.

Whether it was a ploy of Jenny's to put him in a good mood for the conversation they were due to have, he couldn't say but she knew full well that lasagne was his favourite. He checked his watch and decided that he had time for a quick bath before it was ready but he only got halfway up the stairs when there was a triple rap on the front door. He opened it to Gordon Patterson.

'Gaz. What brings you here? Come on in, me ol' mucker,' he said, with a step backwards.

'Wotcha, Kev. How's it going?' Gordon wiped his Doc Martens on the coir welcome mat and stepped inside. He was a big man and not all of it was height. His neck was bollard thick, his shoulders wide and muscular and his thighs were solid like the legs on an Elizabethan banqueting table. But his torso was a bit Henry VIII. He was a couple of years older than Kevin and already losing his hair but his pleasant face showed that he was a frequent smiler. Kevin offered him a beer.

'No ta,' said Gordon, 'better not stop. The missus'll be plating up soon. I just popped in to see if you and Jen fancy going to see the new Beverley Hills Cop movie Saturday night.'

'Saturday? Yeah, sure. Don't think Jen's working but I'll have to check with her. They've got her doing all sorts of shifts these days. Where you thinking of going? Mayford?'

'Nah, we're going down to Brighton. Make a night of it.' Gordon made a rhythmic motion like he was polishing a bench with his backside. Despite enjoying the dance floor, he wasn't a natural on it.

'Great. Yeah I'm sure Jen'll be up for that. You in the pub tomorrow night? I'll let you know then, if you are.'

'I'll probably pop in early for a quickie but it won't be for long. Can't afford to be in there all night these days. Having sprogs is expensive.'

The admission seemed to Kevin like a clarification of his concerns and he was suddenly desperate to learn the secrets of coping with them.

'Um, you sure you don't want a beer?' he said. 'Or a cuppa char?'

'Nah, I'm good thanks mate. Just wanted to ask you about Saturday.' Gordon reached a hand towards the door handle. 'I better get going. Don't want the dog to get me dinner. Otherwise I'll have to eat his.'

'Actually Gaz, there's something I'd like to get off my chest, if you can spare a couple of minutes.'

'Oh. Go on then. Make it quick though. Pedigree Chum's bloody awful,' said Gordon. 'What's up?'

'Well…and this is just between you and me okay? Please, don't even tell Trudy.'

'Okay, mate.' A seriousness infected Gordon's face, ironing out all those little lines that appeared when he smiled. Kevin moved away from the door and perched on the sofa. Gordon stayed where he was but folded his arms across his substantial chest.

Kevin began with what Jenny had told him earlier as he'd pulled on his boots to leave for work. His tone was careful, reluctant almost, as though the stork might have spies everywhere and on hearing the words would report back to HQ and somehow make the possibility a definite reality. As he went on airing his fears about starting a family, the words came easier and aside from his initial outburst of congratulations, Gordon, like the good friend he was, listened intently, nodding and humming his understanding. He didn't seem to mind that Kevin was taking his time and when Kevin had come to the end of his unburdening, Gordon moved to the armchair.

'You know what, mate,' he began, 'when me and Trudy got married we knew that we'd have kiddies at some point. We'd talked about it often enough but we never knew when it was the right time to actually start trying for one. It's not like we made that decision. We couldn't. It's like it was out of our hands. Then, when I came home from work one day and she told me she was pregnant, I tell you, I was scared witless. I was terrified of what having a kid would mean, what it would cost, and well…basically of not knowing anything about being a parent. I mean, could you've imagined, me a dad!'

Kevin listened carefully even though he'd heard much of it before and his empty stomach felt buoyant.

'And as for that boozer of a party girl I married, well, would you've wanted her to be your mother?' Kevin smiled at Gordon's gift of seeing humour in every situation. 'But the thing is, you adapt, you change and you cope. Even with the expense of it all. I mean, look at me. I've got number two coming in a few months and I know it's going to be a bloody struggle, like starting all over again in some ways. But we'll cope and it'll be great. And there are always people around to help, you know? Family. Friends. Personally, I think if you and Jen do have a kiddie, it'd be awesome.'

'You do?'

'Yeah. Just think - our kids will be mates. How great will that be? And perhaps it'll persuade you two to hurry up and send out those wedding invites. We need an excuse for a proper bash.'

The smile suddenly went from Kevin's face. He hadn't even thought of that. Of course, they'd have to get married as well.

'Oh come on, mate,' said Gordon, noticing the change. 'Everyone knows you two are a match for life. It's just a matter of time before you make it official.'

'I don't know about that.'

'Mate, be serious. Look at what you've got. Jen's a cracker of a girl and I reckon she'll be a perfect mum. God, I wish my mum had looked like that.' Gordon made a salacious, Carry-On type of expression, which made Kevin laugh.

'And we're only here to procreate anyway, you know that, don't you? And besides - and I've told you this before - having a kid is the most amazing thing ever.'

'Really?' Kevin was ever so slightly rapt. His eyes were no longer focussed on his friend but on an image his mind had conjured of a possible future, an image of Jenny and him with a newborn baby in their arms surrounded by an aura of happiness that bordered on delirium.

'I know it's something you hear all parents say but it's the God's honest truth. It's hard to put into words but...' Gordon glanced around the room looking for them, 'whatever is the greatest moment in your life so far, times that by ten. By a thousand. Honestly mate.' He rose from his seat. The discussion was over. 'I've got my fingers crossed for you both.'

Kevin rose to see his friend out.

'Not a word, okay?' said Kevin, moving towards the door.

'My lips are sealed, mate.' Gordon reached for the door latch and twisted it open.

It was raining steadily now, pattering on the ground and in the puddles with vigour. 'Jesus. More rain,' he said, standing sideways in the doorway. 'I think you and Jen would do great.'

Kevin didn't know what to say so he didn't say anything. Instead he simply reached for Gordon's hand and gave it a firm squeeze. Not a shake but a firm, manly amount of pressure that conveyed just the right amount of love and respect between friends. The pressure was returned.

'Thanks, mate. You'd make a great salesman.'

'I know. Sell a pair of ballet slippers to a one legged sumo, me.' Gordon stepped out towards his car. He'd parked it directly behind Kevin's van so it was only a few wet strides away. 'I'll see you in the pub early tomorrow!' he called, before sinking into the driver's seat.

'I'll be there.' Kevin called back. 'Hope the dog didn't get your dinner.'

But Gordon had already closed the door. The Vauxhall Astra whined as it reversed back out to the lane, its tyres splashing in the puddles, its headlights yellow in the dusk. And then it was gone. Kevin closed the door and suddenly smelled dinner.

16 October - 2:10 a.m.

Jenny Dwyer pulled on her coat and buttoned it to the neck. A staff nurse recently arrived to start her shift had spoken of gale force winds and rain outside. She'd also joked about Michael Fish on TV assuring someone who'd phoned the Met Office yesterday that a hurricane wasn't about to sweep up the Channel. Jenny balked at the thought of going out in it. Wind and rain together were, without doubt, the worst combination. No wonder England was so green; it was always so bloody wet. But a hurricane? Force ten gales perhaps, but not those great swirling storms that usually batter the tropics.

She closed her locker and pocketed the key but remained fixed to the spot. Her feet were reluctant to move and it wasn't due to the prospect of getting wet. Her vacant gaze held the drab, grey metal door that was less than an arm's length from her face and her eyes became hot and moist. Despair surged upwards into her throat and threatened to overwhelm her but she swallowed it back down like a mouthful of hastily chewed food. If it had been a mirror she was standing in front of she'd have seen tired, worried eyes looking back at her, straw-blond hair pulled tight in a pony-tail, a wide mouth with full but unhappy lips and a serious nose supporting a pale, anxious brow. But the grey door didn't reflect these things. It didn't reflect anything. She didn't even really see it. Instead, she saw her thoughts twirling on a chaotic merry-go-round in her mind.

Conspicuous among them, she saw the arrival of a baby in her life and the departure of the man she thought she would grow white-haired and wrinkly with. One love coming, one love going.

Jenny had known she was pregnant for almost two months now. The first missed period had been enough to convince her because her female intuition told her it was true. Somehow she just felt pregnant. But it was the doctor's appointment last week that told her she could no longer keep it to herself. Now, she had a little miracle growing inside her and fairly soon it would start to push her waistline forward.

She had delayed telling Kevin because she had feared his reaction. There would be finger pointing and raised voices followed by tears and it would culminate with the front door slamming on their relationship forever. Yesterday she had dropped a little hint just before he'd left for work in order to prime him but she had added the little white lie that it was probably a false alarm. Yes, it was wrong of her but at least it'd give him time to think about the possibility. Not that it would make any difference.

It was a heartbreaking shame because in all but this they were perfectly matched but he had never shown any inclination towards wanting kids even in the long term. Whenever the subject had come up - usually in company - he had expressed his opinions as though parenthood was a fatal disease - one that his single-mindedness had permanently inoculated him against. Jenny on the other hand, had always known that she wanted to be a mother, ideally before she hit thirty. This difference between them had initially been a minor concern but she just slid it onto the back burner in the hope that Father Time would simmer away and slowly instil a little paternal yearning in him, particularly once friends started having babies.

Poor Kevin. He was still such a boy in many ways and perhaps at three years her junior, that's exactly what he was. His determination to stave off any adult responsibility, to hold onto his youth for as long as possible had once appeared quite whimsical and endearing but now seemed little more than pitiable. Even persuading him that it was time to move in together had been a struggle for while he had coveted the notion of living alone with her the realities of having to stand up for his own accountability had frightened him. She could see that now as clear as day. But she was going to be twenty-six soon and, recent nights lying awake feeling isolated and anxious beside her man, she'd come to the conclusion that she was ready to become a mother even if the circumstances weren't ideal.

Her brooding was interrupted when the door to the locker room banged against its stop. Cathy Cox, a well-worn middle-aged mother of three who worked on reception bustled in, her plimsolls squeaking on the polished blue linoleum.

'Oh, Jenny.' She seemed surprised as she inserted the key into her locker. 'Thought you'd left already.'

'I'm just off,' replied Jenny, wiping away the tears that were threatening to spill over the rims of her eyes and down her cheeks. She hurriedly picked her bag up from the floor. 'I hear it's not very nice out.'

'I'll say,' said Cathy, rooting around in the pockets of her coat. 'One of the ambulance drivers just came in and said the gusts are strong enough to knock you off your feet. Apparently it's even brought down a scaffolding in Mayford.'

'Really?'

'Uh huh. You be careful driving home.'

'I will.' Jenny pulled her car keys out of her bag and made her way to the front entrance of the hospital, responding to the occasional 'goodnight' from a colleague as she went.

Several people were standing either side of the main doors looking out. One of them whistled in amazement at the weather.

'Careful how you go, Miss,' said a porter, in pale blue coveralls as Jenny passed by. The doors opened automatically as she approached and the wind, howling like a jet engine, immediately tried to force her back inside. Needles of rain hit her face and hands as she moved aside to allow the doors to close behind her. She stood with her back against the wall beneath the entrance canopy shielding her eyes as though from a sand storm. The wind surged and buffeted against the walls of the building in its search for a through route, funnelling along surfaces and whirling out of corners and up towards the eaves, screaming up high through the wires and the aerials. Signposts around the car park fidgeted nervously as debris from bushes and trees skittered across the ground.

Jenny was forced to walk with her head bent into the wind and more than once, she was caught mid-step by a gust that threatened to throw her off balance but she gritted her teeth and battled her way on towards her car.

When she reached it and tried to open the driver's door it felt as though several strong pairs of hands were inside resisting her efforts but with an arm hooked inside and then a drenched leg, she managed to squeeze through and drop down into the seat of her Fiesta. She'd never before experienced a wind as strong and as she sat gathering herself, it whistled against the door mirrors and rocked the little car on its suspension. She pictured Kevin sleeping peacefully in their bed and wished she were there beside him holding his warm body to hers. But then the truth of her newly affirmed pregnancy quickly elbowed that cosy image aside. She sighed forlornly and turned the key in the ignition.

The wind leaned its shoulder against the car as Jenny steered across the open expanse of car park and out onto the road. Twenty yards on and she passed the last street lamp and the orange hue dissolved into the cave-like darkness of the countryside. She'd never really noticed it before, the change from orange to black, but tonight the dark seemed denser than usual as if it needed to hide something terrible from her.

The initial part of her journey home was normally a moment when she would breathe a sigh of relief, a moment where the stress of her shift would begin to leave her tired muscles. The smooth surface of the gently undulating road had a sort of massaging effect on her and with its tall bordering hedgerows giving a limited field of vision like a horse wearing blinders, it presented an idea of simplicity and peace after the multi-directional hustle and bustle of the hospital. But tonight there was no peace and certainly no calm, just a feeling of isolation.

In her high beams the rain surged across the road in dense slashing sheets, so dense that at times it rebounded the car's headlights in the way that fog does. The hedges looked ragged and battered along their tops and in several places, they had lost their integrity altogether and were flopped over. Jenny flinched as bits of flying debris crossed her path and the closer they were to the windscreen, the tighter her grip on the wheel and the harder she bit down on her lip.

Inside the car it was clammy and warm, too warm for a mid-October night, but Jenny was too afraid to lower her window. She felt the need to stay sealed within her little pod of safety, her little metal pod that was being buffeted and blown by these terrible winds. Her wipers, on full speed, swept away the slashing rain and the leaves in a relentless duel and all the while, the wind barged arrogantly against the car, forcing her to make quick adjustments with the steering wheel to keep her line true.

Up ahead beside a wooden bus shelter, an unlit telephone box looked eerie and abandoned and for a second, it made her think of her future again. But it was a thought no sooner in her mind than out again, erased by the sight of the roof on the bus shelter curling up in the wind, unfolding and then lifting clear into the air and over the hedge like a sheet of newspaper caught in a stiff breeze. Jenny instinctively slowed the car and steered to the opposite side of the road, her eyes fixed on what was left of the shelter. The panels that made up the sides twisted and flapped away from their anchors, one slewing across the road ahead of her, another lying helplessly against the phone box like a defeated boxer against the ropes and a third lifting high into the darkness overhead. Jenny let out a shriek and ducked her head in readiness for it to come crashing down onto the car but it didn't and she assumed it must have flown over the hedge in pursuit of the roof.

She was wide-eyed and petrified now and desperate to get home. If the wind was strong enough to rip bus shelters apart and hurl them into the sky perhaps it was a hurricane after all. But hurricane or not, she was acutely aware that danger was everywhere and that it could come at her out of the darkness any moment. Her heart was pounding as she steered around the still-animated panel of the bus shelter and accelerated to an urgent yet cautious speed.

At the junction with the main Mayford Road, a bough from an old oak tree had snapped and fallen onto telephone wires. They were now a tangled and twisted mess on the road amid a seething carpet of green and brown debris.

As Jenny drew alongside she could hear the horrendous wailing of the wind through the leaves and the agonizing groans of the great tree's remaining boughs as they reluctantly bent to the pressures being forced upon them. Falling twigs and dislodged birds' nests rattled down onto the car like hail before a larger piece of tree broke loose and fell onto the rear window with a dramatic thud. Jenny shrieked again and, fumbling with the wheel and the gearstick, steered left out of the junction and took off towards Maydown Common without even looking to see if anything was coming from the right.

Suddenly she was overcome with the sensation that she was completely immersed in danger, as though she had unwittingly swum into shark-infested waters and without even realising she'd started, she found herself repeating a little prayer - 'Dear God, please keep me safe. Please keep me safe.' Her eyes, which were already tired, were now as dry as sandpaper and her intense scrutiny of her surroundings had produced a dull ache behind them. Everything was moving everything was swaying. Everywhere. Left, right, far and near, everything was a potential danger, and Jenny's eyes had to notice it. She had to see it all and then her brain had to process it all. She was so tense she was hardly breathing.

The road uncurled in front of the frightened little Ford as it continued on its way through the churning countryside. All along the crest of the rise that led down towards the village the large detached houses were in darkness. No great surprise considering the hour however, Jenny had got used to seeing the occasional glow in a window somewhere along the way; the comforting night light left on for a child or a reading lamp burning into the wee hours as someone found a book too involving to put down. The pervading darkness was eerie, unnatural almost. But then, whenever Jenny finished the late shift and emerged from the corridors of fluorescent light and antiseptic squeak into a sleeping world where most people were warm in their beds, she thought it unnatural. Tonight though it felt otherworldly too. The thrashing of the foliage and the howling in her ears, the rocking and shoving that she felt through the car seat and the ache in her forearms and shoulders as she struggled with the wheel - it was all alien.

Then, ahead to the right, high up where the beam of the headlights cuts a line out of the dark, Jenny saw movement. Her brain registered it as a threat. Suddenly, the massive crown of a tree came crashing through the front hedge of one of the houses, branches and boughs smashing and splintering on the pavement and across half of the road. Its top bounced several times like a huge head of limp broccoli before it settled but even then it continued to be blown and buffeted by the wind. Jenny cried out in horror and gripped the wheel so hard that her fingers hurt but she didn't slow down. She judged that there was enough room to get past and so she kept going; she had to.

'Please God! Keep me safe. Please God! Keep me safe.'

The entire way in to the village, the road was littered with debris from trees; the smaller bits still moved as if they were alive, the bigger bits rocked in the wind or shifted uneasily where they lay. Some of it was too large to drive over and had to be steered around and Jenny found that she often had to react quickly, snatching the wheel this way or that to avoid an impact with something that flashed out of the dark.

A pair of headlights appeared up ahead, emerging from around a corner in the road. It was such a welcome and unexpected sight that Jenny gasped. All of a sudden the sense of loneliness that had been squeezing the air from her lungs since she'd set off from the hospital left her and she was able to breath a huge sigh of relief. So she wasn't the only person alive in this frightening, unreal world!

The approaching lights seemed to reach out towards her as they drew nearer offering a kind of reassurance like a pair of arms offering a hug. Then she saw the blue flashing light above them and she felt even more comforted. It didn't matter if anything happened now because there were brave, strong men to save her. Jenny slowed the car half expecting them to do the same. But as the fire engine came into the spread of her headlights, Jenny saw the concerned faces of the men in the cab looking down at her with a mixture of astonishment and grief. The fire engine didn't slow down though; it swept past in a roaring, red flash and was immediately swallowed up by the churning darkness behind her. Jenny's fear and her sense of isolation returned and her breath went away again.

When she came to the sign that read MAYDOWN COMMON, a mild sense of relief came back to her because the number of trees along the roadside - particularly big ones - was far fewer through the village. In her mind, this equated to less danger.

But her relief was short-lived. A FOR SALE sign from a Mayford estate agent had blown free from its posts somewhere and was hurtling corner over corner towards her. She shrieked as soon as she saw it flash in the glare of the headlights, instinctively closing her eyes and turning her face away from the impact. A loud clonk went through the car as the board bounced off the leading edge of the bonnet and then went sailing over the roof. Jenny opened her eyes again and shouted out her relief at the near miss.

And she kept going.

'Please God! Keep me safe.'

She was nearly home. Soon she would close her front door, take off her shoes and creep upstairs to bed just as she had done the night before and the night before that. Again she thought of Kevin and wondered if he was tucked up in bed asleep, unaware that she wasn't yet home or if the gales had woken him and got him fidgeting behind the living room curtain waiting for her to arrive. She pictured him there, looking out, frantic with worry and suddenly tears began to blur her vision.

She knew she loved him more than anyone she had ever loved and that in an ideal world, he would be the only man for her yet she was certain she could go on living without him. It would take some adjustment and be painful for a time, perhaps even a long time but she would get over him. But the child growing inside her, the little boy or girl that was as much a part of her as she was of it and would soon be calling her Mama, needed her like the earth needed the sun. Whether in answer to a prayer or simply just through chance, she had now been blessed with a baby and it was her primal God-given duty to nurture it. The child simply would not survive if it weren't for her love and care. She sniffed and quickly wiped her eyes with the back of a hand. She was a mother now and she had a role to fulfil. And she would fulfil it come what may. 'Please God. Help me keep my baby safe.'

As she continued on through the village, Jenny became aware of the indomitable darkness of her surroundings. There wasn't a light on anywhere. The notion that the winds had caused a power cut flashed into her mind and she quickly tried to recall if she had any candles at home in case the electricity was off there too. But such a triviality was difficult to think through with all hell flying loose around her and so she abandoned the query before she'd even mentally opened the kitchen cupboards.

Missiles that she couldn't see continued to clonk, thud and bang against the body of the car. Jenny could see things coming at her from the front and these usually elicited from her reflexes a nervous yank on the steering wheel whether it was needed or not but there were four other sides to her car that were largely indefensible. Surely daylight would reveal hundreds of dents and scratches all over her little powder blue Fiesta.

Everywhere she looked there was damage; signposts leaning drunkenly, others missing altogether; broken roof tiles in the road along with the detritus from the trees. Another tree had come down, this time in the school playground where numerous fence panels had been broken or were no longer there. A Ford Capri parked beside the kerb opposite the school was missing its boot lid and the thin arms of the hydraulic dampers stood vertical and alone, looking puny and redundant now that their reason for existing had deserted them. It all felt so surreal, as though she was driving across a film set, the only cast member in a disaster movie.

At the final corner of the village by the Horse and Groom pub, Jenny turned left into Weir Farm Lane. About a mile further and she would be safe. But now the big trees were back and their great branches swayed menacingly in the headlights. If one fell on the car, she'd be crushed for sure. She knew that. But she also knew there was no alternative for her. There was no other way home that didn't involve driving beneath these great big trees. It was a part of living in the countryside and until tonight it had never been an issue. She just had to keep her wits about her and hope. 'Please God! Keep me and my baby safe.'

Hope has its limitations though and it wasn't long before she came upon trouble. Three hundred yards down the twisting narrow lane her headlights picked out another fallen tree. This time the trunk blocked her path completely, cutting across the road like the body of an enormous serpent. Her heart sank as she drew to a stop but now her fear rose to even greater heights. The noise was horrendous. It was as though the trees were suffering an excruciating death, begging the wind with every last ounce of their energy to stop torturing them. The rattling on the roof of the Fiesta was like an army of bony fingers drumming Jenny out of her wits and, like the layers of an onion being peeled away, the minutes in this terrifying hell were gradually peeling away her composure. She was close to losing control now and as her panic increased, she couldn't find reverse gear and so she began to struggle, to thrash around with the gear stick as though she was stirring some rapidly thickening soup. She could hardly hear the sound of the gears grinding, such was the noise level outside the car but even when she managed to find the gear, the reversing light revealed nothing behind her except a wall of darkness. She was now so tense that she began to shake.

Turning around was her only option and with the wheel on full lock she reversed blindly until the car hit something. She no longer cared about the damage it was sustaining. She was just frantic to get home. She threw it in first and pulled forward on opposite lock. The dense green verge facing her was a seething wall of movement, the branches and twigs of the trees and bushes thrashing and clawing for her. She pulled forward as far as she dare then reversed again without looking back before pulling forward and away up towards the village.

Moments later she had to stop again. In the few minutes since she'd passed by, a large bough had come down and was now blocking her path. She opened her mouth to scream but nothing came out. Her throat was closed tight, barely holding back the hysteria that was swelling beneath the failing crust of her composure. Her eyes were blurring with the tears that were already there.

She was trapped. She was alone. And she was in terrible danger. But she had to keep going. She had no choice.

It felt like she was offering herself with opened veins to the circling sharks but Jenny had to get out to try to move the bough; it was her only option. 'Please God! Keep me and my baby safe.' It was more of a pitiful plea now than a prayer and she found it difficult even to form the words in her mind. Her brain barely had the capacity to think of anything other than the hell that was swamping her.

The wind hooked itself behind the door as soon as she unlatched it and it was yanked out of her hands. It flew round to its limit and made a dreadful grinding sound and then came back with equal speed, almost catching her legs as she stepped out. But she was ready for it with her hands.

Rain and leaves and bits of twig pelted her face as she stood up. It required great effort just to retain her balance because, like a circle of tormenting bullies, the wind assaulted her from multiple directions. She clung to the bodywork of the car as she made her way forward, leaning over like a pensioner with a bad spine while protecting her face with a raised hand. She made it to the bough without falling but it was useless; it was too heavy for her to move. She pushed and pulled with every ounce of strength she had but no matter how hard she strained it wouldn't budge. It was just a stupid, gnarly branch about fifteen feet long and it was all that was stopping her from getting away but she simply didn't have the strength to move it.

The failure finally blew the lid on her emotion chamber and she burst into tears; great wailing sobs that shook her shoulders, loosened her muscles and released her tension. She simply didn't know what to do. Her best just wasn't good enough. And yet she knew she couldn't give up. She had to keep trying, for her and her unborn baby's sake. Despite her streaming tears and the growing sense of hopelessness she tried again to drag the thinner end of the bough around. If she could just make enough room for the car to pass through...

But she lost her grip on it and fell backwards to the road landing awkwardly on some debris. In that instant, as a jolt of pain registered somewhere about her backside, a disturbance in the thrashing wall of vegetation to her left made her scrabble to her feet and move away. In amongst the noise, the banshee howl of the wind, the screaming trees and the suffocating all-round whoosh of leaves and clatter of debris, a deep graunching sound emerged. Jenny didn't know what it was but it sounded bad, like a monster waking from a drugged sleep. She ran up the lane, away from the noise and away from her little car with its little headlights shining through the darkness like the eyes of a trusting friend.

A volley of snaps and pops followed and then suddenly there was a tremendous crash. The noise made Jenny turn round and for a moment she was robbed of the ability to move. She saw the foliage of a tree appear in the road and obscure the Fiesta's lights; glass popped and metal groaned as her little car folded beneath the weight of the trunk. She cried out in sympathy for it but then there was a loud bang that sounded like a gunshot as one of the tyres burst and it shocked her back into flight.

It was virtually impossible to see where she was going now that the headlights had in effect been switched off and so her run became a groping stagger but with her hands outstretched like a zombie and the wind whipping the tears from her eyes, she slowly made her way through the churning, swirling dark.

16 October - 6:08 a.m.

Shortly before 3am, Kevin stirred from his sleep. A shudder went through the house and rattled the sash window in the bedroom but drugged with sleep as he was, he simply thought it was Jenny coming in from work. He was fast asleep again within seconds.

He woke three hours later and was puzzled to find the other side of the bed cold. The familiar red LED digits weren't there on the bedside table and so he fumbled for his watch in the darkness.

It said 06:08.

He sat up and reached for the bedside lamp but soon guessed that there had been a power cut. He threw off the covers and got out of bed, concern racing to his mind as quickly as the damp chill of the bedroom to his skin. He pulled back a curtain and cupped his hands to the glass and the draught around the edges of the sash window tickled his forearms. He couldn't see anything; it was still too dark. But he heard the wind gusting through the leaves of the trees.

Feeling his way around the bedroom, he pulled on his joggers and a sweatshirt and his toes found his slippers. On his way downstairs, he tried the light switch on the landing just to be sure but it confirmed for him that the power was out. Beside the front door at the bottom of the stairs was a row of coat hooks and on one, hung a torch. Kevin lifted it off and switched it on. A circle of light appeared on the wall in front of him making him squint. Jenny's coat wasn't there and neither were her shoes on the doormat. The door remained unbolted too. She had definitely not come home.

Kevin told himself not to worry, that it was fine, that she'd just been asked to stay on at the hospital; something had come up and they'd needed an extra pair of hands. That's all. But wouldn't she have phoned to tell him? His reasoning quickly told him no, not if she'd found out late and decided not to wake him.

He paused briefly to collect his thoughts. He then reached for the phone on the sideboard and lifted the receiver. He held it to his neck with the shrug of one shoulder while he flicked through the address book in the beam of the torch. He found the number for the hospital and dialled but when the receiver met his ear, there was no tone. The phone was dead. He remained still for a few moments, thinking, wondering and his heart beat in his ears.

He heard the murmur of voices outside and a car door close and he rushed to the door. He opened it and the swirling wind entered the room. He shone the torch in the direction of the voices and three neighbours appeared in the circle of the beam. They were standing in the middle of the track. June and Clifford Steptoe from number 1 and Thomas Lamb from number 2 turned their heads to him and their eyes were thin slits.

'Who's that then?' asked Thomas, shining a beam back.

'Kevin. Is Jenny out there?'

'No,' said Thomas. 'Why, didn't she come home?' The man glanced briefly at his companions.

'No. I guess she's still at work. What's going on out there?'

'You mean you slept through it?'

'Through what?'

'Good God, lad. It's been a hell of a night. Come and see this.'

Kevin swapped his slippers for his work boots and, avoiding the puddles, joined his neighbours. The wind whipped around him and played in his uncombed hair and he felt the chill of it around his neck and waist as it whispered beneath his sweatshirt.

'See what?' he asked.

'That.' Thomas raised the beam of his torch to the gutter line at the end of the terrace.

One of the big plane trees that separated Pumphouse Cottages from its immediate neighbour had blown down onto the roof of the Steptoe's house and remained at a forty-five degree angle.

Kevin whistled in astonishment and took a step closer.

'I wouldn't get too close,' said Thomas. 'Damn thing's likely to shift.'

But Kevin took two further steps anyway. He whistled again as his torch beam climbed the length of the tree. The trunk had smashed into the edge of the roof and broken numerous tiles. Shattered roof timbers could be seen through the hole it had made. The metal guttering had broken free of the fascia and was twisted like a sagging ribbon beneath the eaves and in front of number 2. Broken tiles as well as glass were strewn across the ground, but Kevin couldn't see any broken windows because the foliage obstructed most of the first floor of the house. Telephone wires either lay on the ground or tangled within the branches. Kevin drew his beam along the length of the trunk back to its base. The rear quarter of Thomas's Ford Granada was partially crushed beneath the girth of the tree and behind that, the great circle of earth and roots stood exposed, like the wheel of a water mill. Kevin shook his head and went back to the others.

'Were you in bed when it happened?' he asked.

'Of course we were,' said Clifford Steptoe, with mild irritation. He was a short man with a high voice and a nervous disposition. His comb-over was dancing in the wind like the flames of a small fire. 'And I don't mind telling you, it near gave me a blessed heart attack, smashing in through the window as it did.'

June, whose sour face didn't improve even when she smiled, nodded her accord.

'The whole house shook like there was an earthquake or something,' she added. 'And there's broken glass all over the bed.' Her tone demanded sympathy. 'We were very lucky not to be hurt.'

'I'll say you were,' said Thomas. 'You can count your blessing there, and that's for sure.'

'I didn't think it was that windy,' said Kevin. 'It didn't seem to be when I went to bed.'

'Yeah, well according to Michael Fish, there wasn't going to be no hurricane,' said Clifford. 'He got that wrong, didn't he?'

'A hurricane was it?' Kevin asked, with just a hint of scepticism.

'Seems that's what they're calling it,' said Thomas.

'I wonder if there are any other trees down,' said Kevin.

'The radio's saying there's damage all over. Trees down, power lines down, damage to properties. It's pretty bad,' said Thomas.

'And at least three people have been killed by falling trees or buildings,' said June, expanding on what had so far been reported. Kevin's face paled at the news. June noticed and tried to back peddle. 'But I'm sure Jenny wouldn't have attempted to drive home in such a storm. That would've just been silly.'

'What time was she due back?' asked Thomas.

'She finished at two. Should've been home by two-thirty at the latest,' said Kevin. Suddenly, the taste of dread was like bile in his mouth.

Thomas sucked in his breath. 'That's about the time it was all kicking off,' he said, gravely.

'Pity you can't call the hospital to check,' said Clifford.

'Yeah, I just tried. Lines are down.'

'Hmm.'

'I suppose all you can do is wait,' said June, with a wan smile. 'But I'm sure she's fine.'

The two men agreed.

'Anyway, we can't do anything until it gets light,' said Thomas, with authority. He was a stocky man, strong and cheerful and had once owned a small plumbing company. He was easy to like and quick to give an opinion and even though he was retired, he showed no signs of slowing down. 'We can't even get out until this tree is moved and that's a professional's job. I've got a chainsaw in the shed but I wouldn't think about tackling that. Plus we don't know what state the lane's in.'

'Oh God,' moaned June, as if she'd just bitten into a lemon. 'Please don't tell me we're cut off.'

'Daybreak will reveal all,' said Thomas. 'Anyway, I've got a kettle on the stove. Shall we all go in and have a cuppa?'

'Why don't we?' said Clifford.

'Thanks but I'm going to get dressed and head in to the village as soon as it's light,' said Kevin.

'On foot?' said Thomas.

'That or dig out my old bike. I can't just wait around for word. I've got to know if she's all right.'

'Course you have, lad,' said Thomas, patting Kevin's shoulder. 'I'm sure she's fine though. Come on then,' he said, herding the others towards his front door. 'Let's have a brew.' Kevin went indoors to get dressed.

A few minutes before 07:30, the sun broke over the horizon into a muddled sky. Dense pillows of grey and white cloud skimmed swiftly overhead giving way to frequent pockets of cool blue through which the occasional point of a late star could be seen in the western half of the sky. The countryside continued to dance in the wind, swaying and billowing an untidy waltz but it was far less severe than it had been under cover of darkness.

The fifty or so minutes that Kevin had had to wait for daybreak were a torment. Not knowing where Jenny was and whether she was safe harried his mind like the darkest paranoia and he found it impossible to keep still. Without a battery-operated radio, he couldn't get the latest on the news but the horror that had come with June's words '…at least three people have been killed…' filled his head like an acute toothache. Despite his usual morning hunger, he couldn't face the bowl of cornflakes he poured for himself and so he went outside to see if his bicycle was usable. Cycling to hospital would be a lot quicker than walking but either way he was determined to get there as soon as possible.

The narrow rectangle of back garden was a scene of turmoil. Neither Kevin nor Jenny was particularly green-fingered but their garden usually showed evidence that some sort of order was maintained. More often than not it would be Kevin out there, pushing the mower up and down or finding a suitable space to store materials for work but as he stepped out, all order was gone.

Numerous tiles had slid from the roof and lay randomly on the grass, some flat and broken, others stuck in the ground like wafers in ice cream. The buckets and tools that Kevin kept outside the back door were spread all over as if someone had picked them up and tossed them in any and every direction. One bucket still rolled in semicircles in the wind. Jenny's peg basket was halfway to where it'd never been before, dozens of coloured pegs littering the ground and a plastic fertilizer sack had blown in from God knows where. The felt roof of his little shed had come loose in one corner and flapped excitedly whenever a gust caught it and a gap in the fence on the left revealed the panel to be laying on his neighbour's uncut patch of lawn. But right now, none of these things held any importance.

As Kevin half expected, the rear tyre of his bicycle showed flat at the bottom on the floor of the shed. He didn't even bother feeling how soft it was. With little inclination to spend the time fixing it and no idea where the repair kit was even if he wanted to, he decided to walk.

Back in the house he quickly rolled up a couple of towels and arranged them around the base of the fridge in readiness for the impending thaw of the icebox. He rolled a couple of cigarettes and then closed the front door behind him at exactly half past seven. At a glance, his old van looked no more beaten up than it had been the day before which came as some relief. It was covered in twigs and leaves but there were no extra dents on its scruffy bodywork and all the windows were intact.

He felt sorry for Thomas though. His Ford Granada was a nice car and Thomas was the sort of guy who spent his weekends fussing over it. With the tree coming down on its hindquarters, the insurance company would write it off for sure which would be a damn shame. Kevin ducked beneath the fallen tree and set off with some urgency towards Weir Farm Lane and the village.

As soon as he turned onto the lane, he saw further evidence of the night's storm or hurricane, as his neighbours were calling it. The neighbouring group of four large semi-detached houses that stood boldly along the lane had all taken damage to their roofs, missing ridge tiles looking as unsightly against the lightening sky as missing teeth in a smile. Telephone wires had been yanked from their fixings and hung loosely across the lane like wilted liquorice. A car parked on the driveway of one of the houses had a deep creased dent on its bonnet where a tile had fallen. Garden hedges were askew, curled over towards the road like waves about to be surfed and a wheelbarrow was on its side against the opposite verge.

As he walked, Kevin noted that wherever there were trees beside the road, the tarmac beneath was cluttered with the fallen debris of twigs, branches and leaves, all scattered as though a delivery of winter logs had just been stacked away and the sweeping up was still to do. The wind continued rustling fiercely through the heads of the trees and whipped up along the ground often pushing Kevin forward on his toes.

At the next row of cottages, Malcolm Derby was standing in the road taking photographs with his camera. Derby was an insurance man, thin and rangy and sociable.

'Some night, huh?' said Kevin, as he approached.

'You're telling me,' replied Derby.

'Bloody Hell!' A glance in the direction that Derby had his camera pointed gave Kevin a shock. What had been a chimney stack standing four or five feet high on Derby's roof was now a pile of rubble in the front garden. Two courses of brickwork remained around the lead flashing up on the slope of the roof but that was all. A path of tiles several feet wide were smashed where the chimney had slid or tumbled down and the gutter was broken and hanging vertically outside the bedroom window.

'A bit like that, isn't it?' said Derby. 'You should've heard it come down.'

'You all okay though?' asked Kevin 'I bet the girls were terrified.'

'We're fine. The girls slept right through it, can you believe?'

'I did too.'

Derby laughed. 'Much damage up your way?'

'Couple of tiles down but I think that's it for me. The Steptoes in number one have a tree in their bedroom though and Thomas Lamb won't be driving his nice old Granny anymore.'

Derby drew in his breath. 'This'll push premiums up without a doubt. But what else can we do? You off into the village?'

'Jenny didn't come home last night and with the phones out, I've no idea where she is, so I'm going to find out. I'm hoping she's at the hospital.'

'Wow, you've got some walk ahead of you.'

'Yeah, I know. But I've got to do it.'

'Of course you have. You must be worried sick, especially with the news reports. Apparently several people have...'

'Yeah, I heard,' said Kevin, cutting in. He didn't need a reminder.

'Ah. Well, I'd give you a lift if the lane wasn't blocked.'

'Is it?'

'Afraid so. I tried to get down there a little while ago but there's a big tree across the road about halfway down. About where that big barn is, you know?'

'I'll be able to get under it, won't I?'

'Or over it, yes, I should think so.'

'I better get on then. Seeya, Malcolm.'

'Yep. See you.'

About three hundred yards further along the lane, Kevin came to the junction with Weir Farm Lane. The buzz of a chainsaw emerged on the wind, meandering in and out of selected gusts. Any other morning it wouldn't have raised an eyebrow but this morning it signified destruction; another fallen tree, another smashed fence or worse.

At the top of the lane, a five bar gate gave a sweeping panorama of ploughed earth and woodland. Maydown Common lay along a low ridge beyond the tree line but it was just about possible to pick out the spire of St. Joseph's and a roof or two from the eastern edge of the village. Kevin ignored the view and continued on down the lane; his pace urgent, his thoughts unsettled.

Yesterday evening, he'd seen his future and it had made him giddy with happiness. Three cans of Fosters contributed somewhat to the giddiness but the happiness had been genuine. It was the image that he'd conjured up of Jenny and him holding a newborn baby while Gordon waxed lyrical about the joys of parenthood that had been the launch pad for his imagination and it had shot off into the stratosphere like a rocket from Cape Canaveral. Suddenly it all just seemed to click and the images came freely into his slightly inebriated mind.

He saw the birth - though how accurate it was he couldn't testify - and he saw the preparations that came before it. He saw Jenny getting large and moody, eating weird combinations and telling him to keep his hands to himself every time he reached for her in the night. He saw the cot they would buy and the nursery he would decorate and he saw them pushing the child in a pram along the lane on a fine summer's day. And all the while they were smiling.

He saw many other things before he fell asleep because all of a sudden he knew exactly what he wanted. It became all so clear. It was an awakening. He knew he wanted to get married as soon as possible and whether Jenny was pregnant or not.

No more doubts, no more procrastinating, he'd told himself with an impatient clench of the jaw. Just get on with it. Take your damn toe out of the water and dive in, reach out with your arms and pull your future towards you! Gordon was right - Jenny was a cracker of a girl and she would make an awesome mum. Kevin knew that beyond a certainty and he also knew that she was the girl he wanted to spend his life with. It really was as simple as that.

But now, the idea that last night's storm had taken several lives felt like an ulcer attacking the lining of his stomach. The chances of Jenny being one of the unfortunate ones were small, he knew that, but a nagging feeling that life was inflicting on him the biggest possible irony just wouldn't go away. It would be just his luck. Jenny had spoken of having children many times in the past but he'd always refused to entertain the idea. She'd also mentioned marriage but he'd made his excuses about that too. Now that he'd seen the light, so to speak, he was very much afraid that life was about to exercise on him its cruel sense of humour.

Weir Farm Lane was blocked where Malcolm said it was; the tree filled the space between hedgerows with its broken, battered canopy. Not far from the watermill wheel of earth and roots that had until recently been in the ground stood a large barn made from telegraph poles and corrugated iron. It was set back a short way from the lane in the entrance to a field. Several sheets of the iron were missing which revealed the barn to be packed to the beams with great round bales of straw. Beside the barn was where the grand old oak had stood, probably for several centuries. Now though, its future was short and a team of chainsaws would no doubt be along soon to remove it from its home forever.

Kevin found a way through the leaves and boughs, picked his way over smashed branches and scattered debris and continued on down to the mill at the bottom of the lane.

An old brick wall, patched white with lime stain and desperately in need of pointing gave the mill a stout border of privacy from the lane and usually the white-haired former army man Colonel Douglas would walk his black Labradors around his grounds unseen by passers-by. But this morning a fallen tree had breached the wall and the dogs barked and held their tails high at the Colonel's heels as Kevin walked past.

Climbing back up the slope towards the village the number of snapped branches and shattered boughs blocking the road increased. Most could be stepped over or around but a couple were big enough to require straddling. It was a surreal scene; yesterday the lane had been a winding river of tarmac beneath an arched tunnel of green but now, the river was dammed and the tunnel had collapsed.

Up ahead among the tangle of hanging green and fallen debris, a tree had completely cut off the road. When Kevin reached it he had to climb over it but as he slid off the other side he saw a car in the middle of the lane ahead. It was all but obscured by the foliage around it but nevertheless he could see it had been crushed beneath the might of the tree, which had come to rest about four feet from the ground. As he drew nearer his eyes widened and his feet slowed. Suddenly his stomach filled his mouth and, spurred by a torrent of dread, he rushed forward. A dozen feet from the car, he stopped and let out a sickening moan. It was Jenny's Fiesta, crushed like a can of coke under a heel. For a moment he couldn't move, couldn't even breathe as the shock of what his eyes were seeing paralyzed his brain. Then he gasped.

'No. No!' he cried. 'Please God, no!' How could life be so cruel? His stomach lurched and pushed the taste of vomit into his mouth. Pinheads of stone cold sweat broke out all over his body and yet his brain felt as if it were cooking in the juices of its own dread. His legs lost all strength and as he inched closer to the buckled wreckage they seemed to acquire all the stiffness of hot candles. His vision became darker and grainier with each wobbling step and he had to take a moment and steady himself against the tree before ducking beneath its shattered arms.

The Fiesta's doors were open but bent perversely and tiny cubes of shattered glass littered the road like a haul of spilt diamonds. The car looked as though it had died an agonising death and Kevin tried desperately not to picture how it might have been for Jenny.

His throat was brimming with acidic dread. He was going to retch. How could he possibly prepare himself for the sight that was about to greet him? Several times he moved forward to see - because he knew he had to - but each time he had to stop and take a steadying breath. Whatever he was about to see, he would see every time he closed his eyes, probably for years to come.

Then, he wanted to turn and flee, to save himself from this horror, to run back home and hide and to wait for the miracle that would bring her back to him. This wasn't really happening, after all. Was it? But he couldn't run. He had to know. He had to see to be certain. He held a hand to his mouth as he forced himself to look inside the crushed cabin for his girlfriend's corpse. For it would be nothing less. No one could have survived such a thing.

Could they?

Around him, the wind continued to sweep across the countryside in gusts and swirls; the sun shone briefly through a patch in the cloud and then disappeared again behind a large pillow of grey. A chorus of chainsaws had started up and buzzed from the direction of the village.

Kevin had to stoop under the trunk to see inside the car and he very nearly threw up when he saw just how squashed the front seats were. But all he saw through the gaping, misshaped rectangle where the windscreen had been was the shattered dashboard and the checked pattern of the vinyl seats. He edged closer, avoiding the twisted metal of the passenger door. His boots crunched over the glass on the ground.

But he couldn't see Jenny.

He moved around to the driver's side and, ducking low, peered in through the open door at the flattened seat and the terribly compacted roof. She wasn't there! Thank God, she wasn't there. Relief and contrition washed away his strength like a sandcastle swamped by a tide and he had to hold onto a bough to stop himself from sinking to his knees.

After a minute, he moved away and bent over, hands on knees. His vision blurred and his relief dripped off the end of his nose and onto the road. Thank you, God! Thank you. Thank you. Thank you.

When he looked up again, his face had regained some of its colour. There was a faint smile on his lips as well. It wasn't that he was happy because he still didn't know where Jenny was or if she was safe but at least she wasn't going to be an appalling vision of crushed lifelessness in his dreams for the rest of his days.

He wiped his eyes and went back to the car to look for a clue as to what might have happened. He noted that there was no sign of blood anywhere and the car showed no evidence that Jenny had been pulled or cut out by rescuers and this added to his relief. It suggested to him that she had left the car before the tree had fallen onto it and the only reason she would have done that was if she had been unable to go anywhere in it.

With a growing sense of hope, Kevin looked at the bough in front of the car then at the fallen tree a little way behind it. His imagination was joining the dots quickly now, optimism lifting the confusion and mental fog to allow clear thinking. He came to the resolute conclusion that she had got trapped but then run to the nearest shelter.

And that was up in the village.

The shock, the fear and the guilt that, moments ago, had threatened to sweep him away in a tidal wave of tragedy and heartbreak had vanished, replaced by a swelling conviction that his girl, his love was fine. At that moment it became crystal clear that Jenny was everything to him and that without her, he'd be adrift like a yacht bobbing about on a featureless ocean without a crew, without a sail, without a hope. He ran up the lane towards the village, jumping over debris and clambering through the branches of yet another fallen tree.

As the end of the lane came into sight the angry rasps of chainsaws grew louder, an aural indication that the locals were already toiling away to restore access in and out of the village. Kevin guessed that it probably wouldn't be until the end of the day, perhaps even later, before the route back home would be cleared for cars. Around here, there were probably only so many chainsaws to cut and tractors to drag and so those who did own them could expect a busy few days.

Across the junction the white-stuccoed walls of the Horse and Groom glowed briefly in a glance of sunshine as it peered through another hole in the cloud. Kevin considered it logical to start his search there because the pub would have been the first door Jenny had come to.

Stepping up to the solid oak front door, the ulcer in his stomach having hatched into a rabble of butterflies, Kevin noted that the pub had suffered some wind damage as well although it appeared to be only minor. Several roof tiles and hanging baskets weren't where they ought to have been and one of the heavy wooden garden benches lay sprawled like an upturned beetle, legs pointing ineffectually skywards.

Kevin heard his knock resonate throughout the bar within. He considered his explanation to Marv the landlord for knocking so early as the sound of heavy bolts being slid back came from behind the door. He formed his apology and his opening question. The door swung slowly inwards. He opened his mouth to speak. But then he stopped for there she was; looking tired and harassed but more precious than ever. The light, the love of his life.

There was the briefest of pauses fuelled by the surprise that he felt but then they flew to each other like a pair of magnets.

Whatever had been the greatest moment in both their lives so far...well, they could times it by ten or by a thousand.

78

Blast From the Past

'Here you are boys,' said Mr Fenwick, presenting both his sons with a shiny new shilling. 'And I won't need two guesses to know where you'll want to spend it, will I? But remember,' he waved a cautionary finger at them, 'once it's gone, it's gone.' He winked at their beaming faces and the two boys took the coins from his fingers.

'Thank you, Father. Thank you,' they chimed in unison before dashing noisily upstairs to their rooms almost as quick as rabbits down a hole.

'And if you're off where I think you are,' he shouted up after them, 'make sure you're back in time for dinner.'

'Who's going where?' asked Mrs Fenwick, as she emerged from the kitchen in her apron. 'Hello darling,' she added, offering a flushed cheek for her husband to kiss.

'They're off down that exhibition again, I've no doubt,' he said, handing her his hat and cane. The two boys came crashing back down the stairs, all thundering footsteps and squealing voices as they raced past their parents towards the front door.

'Don't be long,' called their mother, moving to the hat stand where she placed her husband's things.

'We won't,' replied Tom, as the door slammed behind them. The squares of stained glass in the leaded lights rattled briefly as the sound of the boys' footsteps on the pavement outside grew fainter.

'You know they'll be gone for hours. They'll miss their dinner,' said Mrs Fenwick, with mild reproach.

Mr Fenwick sighed deeply, contentedly. 'Let them have their fun. They're just being boys. Besides, it won't be there much longer.'

Twenty minutes later and the boys were there; there in the heart of the greatest wonderland of excitement and splendour there had ever been. The King had opened the British Empire Exhibition on St. George's Day that year to great fanfare and together with his son Edward, Prince of Wales, he'd given an important speech - and the first ever radio broadcast by a British sovereign - about how its aim was to promote trade and mutual understanding between all the nations loyal to the British crown. The exhibition sprawled across more than two hundred acres of what had, until recently, been Wembley parkland.

Now though, it was a veritable nirvana. Virtually every colony, dominion and protectorate - fifty-six out of a total of fifty-eight - from around the Empire was represented but to Tom and George, it seemed as though the entire world was there and that each country had brought a little piece of itself to show off.

There were grand, white colonial style palaces from countries like Canada and Australia and exotic pavilions topped with onion-shaped domes and tall minarets from places like Malaya and India. There was a whole village of thatched huts within a walled city representing the countries of West Africa and from Hong Kong, an entire Chinese street where traders sold carvings, toys and silks and such like. Each nation had organised displays of their produce and their wares, much of which could be bought, and everywhere Tom and George looked there was something they'd only ever seen before in the pages of an encyclopaedia.

Housed within two enormous new concrete buildings - the largest of which was even bigger than the neighbouring Empire Stadium where the previous year's F.A. Cup Final had been won by Bolton Wanderers - were the vast exhibits from Great Britain, where almost anything one could think of from the fields of engineering and industry, from horticulture and the arts were displayed proudly to the rest of the world. The stadium itself, which had just been finished in time for the cup final, was used for spectacular shows including pageants, concerts and even a Wild West Rodeo Championship.

There were lakes and gardens, restaurants and cinemas as well as a bandstand inside an amphitheatre. And to ferry the visitors around the massive site there was a non-stop miniature railway and a sort of electric tram system called a Railodok.

The boys had already been several times before and yet they still walked slowly along the thoroughfares, awestruck with every sight and sound. It was simply too exciting to chance missing even a single thing. And yet as eye-catching as all this was, they weren't going to stop until they reached the amusement park.

Once there, they were in heaven. Every few paces brought forward a different tune of jolly organ music and every few paces filled their noses with an aroma that made their mouths water - the sweet, warm tang of candyfloss and doughnuts and fresh baked cookies or the savoury temptation of fried potato chips.

'Wow, it's just amazing in the dark,' admitted George breathlessly, his eyes standing out on stalks at the kaleidoscope of colours that flashed and twinkled in every direction.

'It sure is,' replied his brother. 'I've never seen so many lights. It makes Piccadilly look quite dull.'

Hundreds of people milled around the park, and the numerous side stalls and penny arcades were chock-full of them trying their luck for a little prize. Along with the organ music, the warm, early evening air was alive with the shrieks and screams of those who were enjoying the rides they had come to see - the bumper cars, the helter-skelter and the carousel among them. Beneath these sounds of delight were the low-down hums and rumbles and occasional clatters of mechanical motion as the hidden gears and belts and chains that drove the rides toiled away.

The owner of a shooting gallery called out to the boys as they went by, offering one of his little pellet guns and daring them to try their chances but the boys declined - they knew exactly where they wanted to go.

The Giant Racer was the jewel of the park and the boys wanted to spend their shilling there. They passed the strange Oriental-style turrets of the Burmese Pavilion and then came to the huge, fake mountain that featured at one end of the giant rollercoaster ride. A Union Jack, rising from the mountain's apex, fluttered gently in the evening breeze, its red, white and blue picked out by the bright beams of three spotlights.

The huge wooden framework of the rollercoaster structure was lit from the ground and from lamps positioned at certain points along the route and in a few places, it must have been   fifty or sixty feet high. With their hearts thumping in their chests, the boys gave their fares to the man at the entry gate and were ushered straight into a car by an attendee.

'What luck, no waiting. You got the paper?' Tom asked, as they secured the safety bar in front of them.

'Yep,' said George, excitedly unfolding a newspaper from his trouser pocket.

'Ok, you first, then me, all right?' said Tom.

Moments later, the remaining cars were filled and with a jerk, they were off. Chains clanked and rattled as gears dragged the wooden cars up the first steep incline. The park spread out below them like a sparkling, golden sea of light and magic and as they gained height their anticipation soared. Shouts and cheers erupted from the passengers as the cars finally levelled out and they all looked down in awe at the view and then...

Suddenly, the cars seemed to leave the rails and fall vertically and a dozen pairs of lungs emptied as screams filled the air. The cars hurtled down the tracks with a rapid clickety-clack as necks were whipped and strained against the forces.

George held the folded newspaper in one hand against the bar and tried to read a sub-headline. The rush of wind filled his mouth and blew out his cheeks so that he couldn't even form the first word and he burst out laughing. He tried again as they sped into a sharp right-handed turn but it was such a violent change of direction that after just five juddering words, his eyes were unable to focus on the print. Again, he laughed out loud. Tom, who was howling at his brother's efforts, took hold of the newspaper as they went up another steep incline.

'See if you can do better,' shouted George, his sides aching with joy. The train reached its peak height again and slowly turned a corner. Tom began to read as they plummeted down a slope and he managed an entire sentence before they reached the bottom of a dip, shot back up again and skewed around a curve. Their speed and the harsh vibrations of the car made it impossible to keep his eyes fixed on the print and he'd lost his place within a few seconds. They both tried one more time but their efforts were hilarious and as the ride came to an end, their eyes were streaming and their jaws and ribs ached from their laughter.

'Again?' asked George, looking at his brother's windswept hair.

'You bet,' answered Tom.

That Extra Mile

The train eased into the station and came to a rest beside the platform. Anthony Alcott, tall, heavy around the middle and greying in an agreeably distinguished way, peered out at the rain. The term stair rods came to him and he offered a light-hearted warning to his wife who was standing behind him.

Melissa groaned her displeasure and peered around her husband's shoulder.

'That's what happens when you bring a handbag that doesn't have room for an umbrella,' she said, her voice as clear as a radio newsreader's but infused with the sarcasm of a wit. 'How far along the platform have we stopped?'

'Far enough to get wet, my dear,' replied Anthony, with a facetious grin. It was late in the evening but he still looked immaculate in his evening suit and dress shoes. He glanced down at his wife's strappy sandals and smiled. 'You run in those?'

The doubt in his tone offered a challenge to Melissa.

'Just watch me', she stated, with a defiant tilt of her head.

A few hours ago, they had been enjoying a warm August evening in London; so warm, that Melissa was glad she had chosen not to bring the shawl that went with her dress and also so beautiful, that they had decided to walk from the theatre to Trafalgar

Square where they had then taken a taxi to Victoria station. Covent Garden had simmered with the lazy babble of evening diners and the delicate rattle of silverware and porcelain.

But then, travelling swiftly through the inky void of the countryside, the only clue to the change in weather had been the streams of water that bobbed across the carriage windows like nervous little worms. This hadn't gone unnoticed by the Alcotts but then it hadn't been given much thought either. Now though, as Anthony lowered the window and reached out to open the door, he took a moment to ready himself as one often does before tackling something unpleasant.

Along the platform, puddles bubbled under the intensity of the downpour, the rain drumming down like pellets on the ground and clattering on the station roof. It created an extraordinary din. Anthony took his wife's hand as they dashed and splashed the twenty or so yards along the platform until they were sheltered by the station's canopy. A young couple also leaving the train made the same mad dash, his jacket pulled over his head, her handbag held aloft.

'Lawks-a-mussy! That, my dear, is what you call rain,' exclaimed Anthony, with an enthusiastic burst of laughter. 'Good God! It's quite a spectacle when it's this heavy, isn't it?'

'Hmm,' grumbled Melissa, showing far less appreciation for the deluge. 'I'll wait here while you get the car,' she said. Like the other woman leaving the train, she too had held her handbag high in an attempt to preserve her appearance but it had done little good. Her elegant hairstyle had swiftly been transformed into a facsimile of a beaver's lodge.

Far along the platform, the guard's whistle came at them through the rain like a child's screech. There was a puff and a hiss as the hydraulic brakes released their grip and a clank from the couplings; then the train moved slowly out of the wet, shiny station and away into the night. The young couple clutched one another closely beneath the inadequate span of a flimsy pink umbrella and, after bracing themselves, moved off giggling in the direction of the car park. The long vertical spears of rain welcomed them like parting curtains and then closed again behind them as if wishing to keep their movements secret from onlookers.

'Perhaps I'll wait a few moments,' said Anthony, his admiration for the violent downpour having evaporated. 'It might stop soon.'

'And it might not and we could be here for hours,' observed Melissa, with a hint of irritation. She nudged her husband in the ribs. 'Go on with you. It's only rain.'

'That's easy for you to say. You're not the one who'll get soaked.'

'Oh, don't be such a baby. You can have a nice bath when we get in.'

'You'll be sorry when I catch pneumonia and you have to spend your time nursing me back from the brink of death,' said Anthony. And then he was gone, dashing through the downpour, polished dress shoes splashing through the surface water.

Less than a minute later he slid into the dry, leather-lined cocoon of the Daimler. He was dripping water and his trousers clung to his legs like wet bandages; his feet felt cold and oily inside his shoes and a trickle of discomfort traced a line down his spine.

The rain was drumming on the roof with such intensity that when Anthony turned the key, he couldn't hear whether the engine had started. But the little display of lights on the dash did their usual thing and the rev counter needle roused itself from zero and so he slid the gearstick down to D and moved out towards the ticket office. He pulled up a few seconds later and adjusted the heating controls to clear the windscreen, which was already beginning to mist up. Melissa yanked open the passenger door and clambered in, bare legs and arms glistening damp. Her sapphire blue dress was peppered with dark spots and there were big wet patches on the shoulders and down the front where the rain had caught her as she'd run. Her beaver's lodge now resembled a weeping willow.

'Ugh! What ghastly weather,' she cried, slamming the door.

'Ha! My word! You positively look like a drowned rat.'

Melissa pulled down the sun visor and groaned at her reflection in the vanity mirror.

'Yes, well you don't look so smart yourself,' she replied, looking across at her husband's shiny face and his wet hair pasted firmly onto his scalp and down his forehead like a greasy toupee. Anthony looked at himself in the rear-view mirror and guffawed.

'Really, you mean you don't like it? And there I was thinking of changing my look.'

'I'd be quite happy if you changed it, dear,' said Melissa, her tone nonchalant, her grin playful. 'Just don't change it to that.'

'Touché,' said Anthony. The Allcots often teased each other with mock acerbic banter and light-hearted jabs; it had been a part of their relationship from the very beginning and they both knew a winning quip when they heard one. This time, Melissa had managed to have the last word.

When the mist had cleared from the windscreen and a little heat started coming from the vents, Anthony turned the wipers onto their fastest setting and steered the car out onto Station Approach. Melissa pulled off her wet sandals and started massaging her cold, damp feet.

They hadn't travelled half a mile before the downpour eased to a moderate sprinkle.

'That's just typical,' said Anthony, reducing the speed of the wipers. 'I told you we should've waited a few minutes. And to add insult to injury, the rain has…' He squirmed in his seat and let out a miserable moan, 'just…reached…the family jewels.'

'It's a wonder it could find them.' Melissa grinned at her husband.

'Ha ha. Very funny.'

'I know,' she said, with amusement. 'But never mind, you can have that bath soon.'

There was a long pause and then Anthony said with no hint of playfulness, 'A wet end to an otherwise wonderful evening.'

'Wasn't it,' agreed Melissa, as she ran her fingers through her long, damp hair, combing the wavy ends back over her head so that she now looked more like she'd stepped from a shower instead of having just been caught in one. 'Loved that restaurant. Wonderful meal. Probably the finest duck I've ever had.

Definitely go there again. Oh, and your Black Forest Gateau…'

'Yes, that was mighty, wasn't it? Glad you helped me with it, though. I wouldn't have managed it on my own.'

'And the show was so much better than I was expecting. I think that Andrew Lloyd Webber chap is quite a talent. I don't know who that Paul Nicholas is though, but my word, can he sing.' She paused for a moment, remembering. 'That was such a thoughtful birthday surprise from Joshua. I do hope he didn't spend too much on the tickets.'

'They were good seats,' said Anthony. 'But I think perhaps he had a little help in getting them.'

Melissa reached across and gave her husband's hand a grateful pat. A glow of contentment settled on Anthony's face and he let out a rich, soothing, sigh.

For a few minutes they drove on without a word, wet and tired but content. The soft thrum of the car and the intermittent squeak of the wipers as they swept the rain from the screen were the only sounds. The headlights peeled back the darkness from their leafy surroundings turning undefined shadows into three dimensional greenery and every once in a while a car would come towards them with a flash of light and a swish of tyres.

'I think perhaps I'll join you in that bath,' muttered Melissa, in a way that suggested she was merely thinking aloud. Anthony half-turned his face towards her, his expression a mixture of puzzlement and cautious optimism.

'Yes,' she continued, keeping her eyes on the road. 'I think you deserve a nice back scrub. And besides, I need warming up too.'

'A fitting end, I think,' grinned Antony, with a hint of a leer. His eyes rested momentarily on his wife's legs and he pumped his eyebrows.

'Ha! Trust me,' replied Melissa, with a shake of her head. 'After the day we've had, we'll be out as soon as our heads touch those pillows. Nice thought though.'

'Hmm. You're probably right,' agreed Anthony, happily releasing the prospect without the slightest fuss. At that moment, a yawn took hold of him, which at first he tried to stifle. But like a river breaching its dyke, it swelled until it was too much to hold back and so he gave up on that too and let it overpower him. It stretched his jaw to its limit, brought tears to his eyes and culminated in a great, satisfying groan. Melissa smiled and then very soon, yawned herself.

A little way ahead, a signpost beside the hedge pointed the way to Poe; a single black 3 against the white paint revealed its distance. The Alcotts cottage was a little closer than that but required a bit of meandering from the direct route. Anthony slowed and the indicators' orange flashes illuminated the verge.

As they straightened out of the turn, the headlights revealed a pair of leather-clad figures pushing a motorbike up the lane towards them. They both still wore their helmets presumably as protection from the rain. They raised their gloved hands to the glare of the lights until Anthony dipped his high beam.

'That's bad luck,' said Anthony.

'And what a night for it to happen,' added Melissa.

'Shall we see if we can help?'

'Do you know them?'

'No, but should that make a difference?' Anthony's tone was mildly condescending and before Melissa could answer, he drew up alongside the pair, lowered his window and asked if they needed help. Chilly, damp air entered their snug saloon and curled itself around Melissa's exposed limbs. There was a substantial pause before Anthony received a response; it seemed as though the bikers, who were little more than shadowy outlines beside his window, were startled that someone was good enough to stop at such a time and ask after them.

'Can you believe? We are out of petrol,' said the one closest to the car. His voice was muffled beneath the full-face helmet but Anthony thought he detected a foreign accent.

'Bad luck,' replied Anthony. 'And in this weather. Can we give you a lift to a petrol station? I'm not sure where we'll find one open at this time of night but we'll find one somewhere.'

'Anthony!' Melissa whispered sharply in protest. 'What are you doing?'

Anthony didn't respond to her for he knew they'd be no point. He was in a good mood, he'd had a great evening and he was feeling charitable. Here was someone who looked as thought they needed help and, while he might not have usually offered it, tonight he felt like doing so. Simple as that.

He waited for a response to his question. The two bikers moved their helmets close together and quietly discussed the offer like doubles tennis players whispering about their strategy for the next point. After a moment, the first biker said that a lift to the nearest railway station would be the most helpful thing.

'If that's what you want,' replied Anthony. He thought it an odd decision but at least he wouldn't have to drive around searching for an open petrol station. The nearest one would probably be halfway up the A21.

The bikers mumbled some more between themselves, pointing and gesticulating back down the lane and then they turned the little blue Yamaha around and scooted down to a gateless field entrance about thirty yards back. They were both dressed the same with black motorcycle jackets, denim jeans, and black boots. They had matching khaki backpacks but different coloured helmets - one white and one yellow. And they both looked absolutely soaked.

Anthony raised his window and resealed the cocoon.

'Are you sure about this?' asked Melissa. 'They could be anyone.'

'Come on, darling. It's a couple of kids who've run out of petrol. Besides, it'll only take a few minutes.' He eased the Daimler down the lane after the two bikers.

'You don't know who they are?' said Melissa, in a cautionary tone.

'Can you only help people you know, then? Come on Mel, I'd want someone to stop for me if I'd run out of petrol. Wouldn't you? What's the worst that can happen?'

'I don't know.' said Melissa, her voice shrinking, betraying her concerns. 'I'm uncomfortable with this Anthony.'

Through the windscreen they watched as the bikers disappeared into the field then re-emerged moments later without the bike. They no longer had their helmets with them either. They shrugged off their backpacks while shielding their eyes from the headlights as Anthony turned the nose of the Daimler into the entrance. Then, as he slipped the car into reverse they slipped in through the rear doors.

'This is very kind of you,' said the first biker, as they settled into the dark corners of the back seat. The sharp reek of cigarette smoke clung to their wet leathers like a mould and Anthony knew that his wife, who loathed smoking with a passion, would be repulsed by it. He could almost feel her discomfort reach across and slap him for allowing - what she no doubt considered - an unpleasant and equally unnecessary intrusion.

'Do you not want your helmets?' asked Anthony.

'No, we leave them with the bike,' said the first biker.

'Won't they get wet?' added Anthony, with a quizzical frown at his wife, who had assumed a subtle sideways position in her seat, which looked both awkward and uncomfortable.

'They're okay,' said the first biker. 'They won't get wet.'

'You're quite sure?'

'Thank you for this,' he said, ignoring Anthony's undue concern for their helmets. 'We were wondering what we were going to do. It's not a good night to be stuck out here, is it?' The man's voice was cheerful and gracious and possessed a quality that reminded Anthony of Charles Aznavour although his accent wasn't at all French. But he came across as a nice kind of fellow.

'I've no doubt. Not much help to be found out here, I'm afraid,' said Anthony.

Anthony reversed the car and then accelerated up to the main road. As he pulled out across the junction he asked his passengers where they had come from and where they were going. It was the same biker who answered. The second one, the one sitting directly behind Anthony, remained as silent as a monk who'd taken a vow.

They had apparently been at a party in Hastings and foolishly attempted a cross-country short cut on their way back to London. It hadn't occurred to them that they might be low on petrol.

'You should've stuck to the A21,' said Anthony. 'You would've passed any number of petrol stations there.'

'I know that now,' said biker number one, with a little laugh.

'Actually, I think our son was going to a party in Hastings tonight,' added Anthony, as an afterthought. 'Wasn't he, dear? Bit of a coincidence, wouldn't you say?'

Melissa hummed an affirmative. She then turned in her seat and asked, 'What about your friend?' All she could see of the second biker sitting behind her husband was a faint impression of his facial features and the outline of his head against the faint red glow from the car's rear lights. His hair looked to be about collar length and a little curly. 'Is he all right? He seems awfully quiet.'

The second biker seemed to fidget under her gaze, fingers scratching stubble, knees nervously bumping against the back of Anthony's seat.

'He's ok,' said the first biker. 'His English is not so good and he's shy to try speaking the little bit he does know.'

'Oh. Where's he from?' asked Anthony.

'Greece. We both are. But I've been living in London for almost ten years. He's just here on holiday.'

'I shouldn't think he's here for the weather, though,' said Melissa, her chilly discomfort thawing just a fraction.

'No, nobody comes here for the weather, do they?' laughed the first biker.

The Alcotts exchanged glances and Anthony smiled encouragement at his wife as they continued on towards the station.

'So, what do you do in London?' Anthony asked.

'I'm a student.'

'Studying?'

'English.'

'I must say your English sounds rather good,' said Melissa. 'How long have you been speaking it?'

'Ten years almost. As long as I have been here.'

'Oh, of course.'

A few minutes passed in silence but then biker number one asked whether the trains to London would still be running.

'Good question,' replied Anthony. 'I can't answer it because I really don't know. But if they aren't, I'm sure there's a public phone box there so that you'll be able to call someone to come and get you.'

'Ah.' The biker sounded disappointed.

Anthony and Melissa exchanged another look. They each knew what the other was thinking; that these two bikers might ask to be taken further afield, that they might insist on not being left at a station where no trains would be running until the sun came up. In the glow of the dashboard, they saw in each other's eyes the hope that it wouldn't come to an outright refusal on their part, which might then lead to an argument. Suddenly the offer of a good deed had the prospect of turning into an unpleasant situation and Anthony felt a twinge of regret. Five minutes later though, he pulled into Station Approach and drew up outside the entrance to the platforms.

'Here you are,' he said, relieved but at the same time dreading the request that might be on the biker's tongue. However, no sooner had the car come to a stop than their two passengers were out the doors and heading through to the platform, a hasty thanks tossed over the shoulder of the first biker as he slammed the door behind him. Neither man made the effort to turn and wave.

Relieved as they were, the Alcotts were a little surprised that their good deed hadn't received more appreciation; maybe not a handshake but a thank you said with genuine feeling would have been nice.

'Well, that was odd,' said Anthony, staring after the two men. 'And a little rude.'

'They were foreign, my dear,' said Melissa, as if that explained it. She gasped in relief as she repositioned herself in her seat. 'But that was extremely unpleasant. God, what a smell!'

'Yes, that was unpleasant, I'll grant you. But, as I told you,' said Anthony, trying to mask his relief, 'just a couple of kids who'd run out of petrol. Nothing more. And certainly nothing sinister.'

'I doubt they'll get a train,' said Melissa, ignoring her husband's dig. 'Not at this hour.'

'He seemed friendly enough, though,' said Anthony, still looking over his shoulder. 'I didn't get a look at them though. Did you?'

'No. It was too dark.'

There was a brief pause.

'Well, come on,' said Melissa, with an impatient flourish of her hands. 'Let's go before they discover there aren't any trains and come back.'

'I'm going, I'm going,' said Anthony, turning the wheel.

When they once again took the left turn to Poe and passed the spot where the motorbike was hidden, Anthony commented on the strangeness of the bikers' decision to catch a train rather than to find a petrol station.

'In this weather?' asked Melissa. 'I know how I'd prefer to get up to London.'

'Yes, my dear, but it just means that they'll have to come back down tomorrow. And it's hardly just around the corner, is it?'

'That's the choice they made.'

'I know. But it doesn't really make sense. Not to me.'

'Well, I wouldn't fret. There are many things that don't make sense to you,' she said.

'That's true,' agreed Anthony. 'Like why wouldn't you take your helmets with you?'

'Hmm.' Melissa didn't want to think about it. She was just glad they were no longer in her car, filling her mind with unease and her nose with that dreadful tobacco smell. The bike along with their helmets, whatever they'd done with them, she couldn't care less about.

'Hmm, indeed. Oh well.' Anthony sighed deeply, as if drawing a line through the matter. 'Still up for that bath? I think I need a good, warm soak.'

'I'll see how I feel once I get indoors.'

'I know what you mean. I'm about done too.'

For the remainder of their journey, which lasted just over seven minutes, there was no more talk. The prospect of soon being in a nice warm bed lulled them both into a comfortable silence. Anthony threaded the Daimler through the dark country lanes until they turned into the driveway of their cottage. Melissa pulled on her stiff, damp sandals again.

'Ah, thank God,' sighed Anthony. 'One thing about going anywhere, it's always bliss to come home.'

Up ahead, the porch light shone a friendly welcome as they scrunched across the gravel. A narrow wedge of light showed through drawn curtains in a downstairs window.

'Oh! Looks like Josh is home,' said Melissa.

'I thought you said he was staying with Kate tonight after their party.'

'That's what he told me.' Melissa then made a sound that usually accompanies the rolling of one's eyes. 'Oh, I do hope they haven't had another falling out.'

'Now, now mother. Maybe they simply changed their plans.'

'They're always arguing. It's not good. I tell you, if she's the one for him, I do hope they get over this habit of arguing. It's really not healthy.'

The headlights of the Daimler washed over their son's red Escort as they swung up around the curved driveway. Anthony pulled up alongside it and killed the ignition. The Daimler immediately began ticking as it started to cool, fluids settling, pressures easing, metals contracting. Its job was done for the day and soon it would be as cold as a stone.

Anthony and Melissa took a moment to enjoy the feeling of having just landed; London seemed a long way from their quiet, dark driveway and with the comfort of bed just a few steps away, their relief that the long day had finally ended heightened their exhaustion. They both yawned luxuriously, first Anthony and then Melissa.

The rain was much lighter now, no more than a heavy mist and as they stepped into the recess of the porch, their movements were stiff and awkward inside their damp clothes. Anthony unlocked the door and followed Melissa into the unlit hallway. She flicked on a light and he locked the door behind him.

'I think I will have that bath,' he said. 'Just a quick one. I need it.' He shrugged off his damp jacket.

'I'm just going to check on Josh and then I'll come, all right?' said Melissa, prizing off her stiff sandals and heading barefoot into the living room where the light was on.

Anthony took off his shoes and left them beside the door. He was about to head upstairs when Melissa called for him. Her tone surprised him; it was tense and urgent; it wasn't asking him to call back, it was telling him his presence was required.

He went to her and found her kneeling over Joshua, who was face down on the carpet between the furniture. Some magazines and a heavy onyx cigarette lighter from the coffee table lay scattered beside him. Joshua was groaning as Melissa helped him into a sitting position. His cheeks were milky and there was a shiny red circle on the left side of his forehead.

'What on earth's the matter with him?' Anthony's tone was indignant. 'Don't tell me he's drunk again.'

'I don't know yet,' said Melissa, carefully brushing the curls of her son's fringe aside. 'Are you okay, my darling? He's got an enormous bruise on the back of his head.'

Anthony rolled his eyes and said, 'For goodness sake, Mel, stop fussing over him. It's his own fault if he drinks too much.'

Melissa paid no attention to her husband's comments and remained totally sympathetic to her son's condition. Joshua's eyes tried to rest on his mother's face.

'I think he's dazed. Joshua darling, what happened?' she asked. Joshua was solidly built like his father, but without the gut, and his boldly patterned shirt pulled against the swell of muscle in his arms and shoulders as he reached a hand to the back of his head. He found a tender spot and cried out. Melissa winced.

'My poor darling. I think we should put some ice on that.'

'I hope you didn't drive home in that state,' said Anthony, his brow pulled down in disapproval. 'You're old enough to know what could happen.'

'I haven't been drinking,' said Joshua feebly, his voice seeming to come from another room. He looked past his parents and his nut-brown eyes became quizzical. 'Someone was hiding behind that door.'

'What are you talking about?' demanded Anthony, his eyes following Joshua's to the living room door. Joshua pulled himself up and eased onto the sofa. Melissa sat beside him, fussing with her eyes and her hands.

'Someone was hiding behind that door,' he stated, with a little more vigour. 'When I came in, they hit me and…I guess, knocked me out.'

'Are you sure?' Melissa's tone was incredulous yet coaxing.

'I didn't crack myself on the back of the head, if that's what you're saying.'

Melissa looked up at her husband, who was now scanning the room warily.

'You think we've been burgled?' she asked.

'What else?' he replied, coolly. 'Doesn't look like they've disturbed much in here.'

Melissa turned back to her son. 'Did you see who it was?' Her voice was now a whisper.

'No, I didn't, mum. I didn't see anyone; just a flurry of movement out the corner of my eye, that's all.' He frowned with the effort of trying to recall. 'All I know is, I came in here and got clobbered from behind.'

'I think we'd better call the police,' said Melissa, half to herself. 'Let me get you some ice for that bump. Or perhaps a bag of frozen peas would be better. I think I have some.' She got up.

'Wait here. I'd better have a look around,' said Anthony, straightening himself to his full height and squaring his shoulders. 'They might still be here. You didn't see who it was?' he asked again.

'No. But there was a motorbike outside when I came home. A little blue Yamaha.'

Anthony and Melissa looked at each other as their son slowly continued talking through his pain. 'I thought it was a bit odd, sitting out there on the drive with no one around. It didn't occur to me that someone might be in the house.'

Resisting a Rest

Vera Giddy is sitting on an old wooden stool with an elbow on the counter and her chin resting in a cupped hand. She is contemplating retirement and her daydreaming softens the lines of worry along her brow. Her fine white hair has the look of candyfloss and her watery blue eyes normally keen and interested, are vague in their focus.

Retirement is a troublesome topic for her and it has started intruding upon her thoughts with increased regularity now that her sixtieth birthday has appeared on the horizon like a storm front on an otherwise clear, temperate day.

The idea of not having any work to occupy her time horrifies her enormously because ever since she was a young girl Vera has known the sweat and blister of a day's toil. Helping her mother with many of the household chores may have been a long time ago but all that scrubbing, washing and cooking for a family of seven had moulded her young clay and toughened her up both physically and mentally. It instilled in her an ethic of honesty and integrity that has held her in good stead her entire life and even now, all these years later, Vera would admit with her hand on her heart that she likes working and considers it a necessary exercise for a healthy soul. To her - the devil finds work for idle hands - is more than just a short, over-used phrase; it is a fact, a simple God's honest truth, one that she too is fond of repeating every time the news reports someone doing something they shouldn't.

She is also fond of saying - they'll have to carry me out of here in a box - when anyone brings up the subject of what she might do when she eventually calls it a day but she knows this is merely hyperbole. Still, the thought of suddenly having nothing of importance to do, no task to occupy her hands or her mind between the four points of her day's compass - breakfast, lunch, dinner and bedtime - does not give her comfort.

On the other hand, Vera imagines retirement to be a peaceful, gentle time earned through a life of hard work, a time when one can reflect upon one's life; a time to relive happy moments captured on film by sifting through the boxes of old photographs and slides that lay beneath a pall of dust in the attic; a time to write long, news-giving letters to relatives not seen for decades, cousins and nephews that have made their homes in distant cities and foreign countries.

Retirement, she knows, should also be a time for enjoyment; a time when the days will finally be hers to spend any which way she chooses. She can see more of her precious daughter and her beautiful grandchildren and spend more time with her dear friends from the village. She could even take up a hobby - although which one exactly she hasn't a clue - and she could visit all those places she has dreamed about, both at home and - if she could be bothered to apply for a passport - abroad.

Trouble is, all those dreams of retirement travel had been done with Stan, her husband of twenty-seven years. Their dreams of standing alongside the great manmade wonders of the world, of seeing breathtaking scenery in lands where English was not necessarily the first language, had been done as a couple. They had even considered a round-the-world cruise. Oh, the places they would have seen together and the times they would have had. Their golden years would have been so special.

The memory draws a sigh from somewhere deep inside her and Vera gets down from her stool and goes out the back to make some tea. Before she reaches the kettle the shop doorbell tinkles.

'Mornin', Mrs Giddy.' It's Mr Farnham with her egg order and his jovial voice rising and falling in scales as though he is almost singing the words brings a flurry of cheer into the little shop. He approaches the counter with two trays of eggs balanced confidently on an upturned palm. He is short and stocky, like Ronnie Corbett but without the glasses and he moves in a curiously fidgety way. He is wearing dark, baggy trousers, which are a little dusty and held up with red braces and an old shirt with a granddad collar. 'Here y'are. Three dozen, as usual.'

'Thank you, Mr Farnham,' replies Vera, as she takes the delivery from him as well as the receipt he offers with his other hand. 'You don't look very wet. Has it stopped raining?' Her speech is delicately rural and unhurried and her manner is gracious and warm.

'It has for the moment. Though, whether it'll clear up is hard to say.'

Vera is never wanting for a weather forecast. Virtually everyone who enters her shop offers an up-to-the-minute report and an opinion of where it might be going, which is often handy when she has washing on the line in the garden or some that needs hanging out.

'Good Heavens! What on earth are you feeding your hens? They must have been in pain laying these.'

'Be honest,' says Farnham, taking off his cloth cap and scratching his balding pate which had the shine and colour of a prizewinning onion, 'I've no idea what's goin' on with 'em. It might be the weather or their age, maybe even their mood, but I certainly aren't feeding 'em any different. Beautiful size though, aren't they?'

'I'll say. Just one would make me an omelette.'

'Huh, not sure I'd dirty a pan for just one egg, Mrs Giddy,' says Farnham, as Vera rings up a nought on the till and takes out his payment.

'I expect like most men, your size makes no difference,' she says, passing him the money. 'You can all eat for England. I know my Stan could.'

'Hard work needs fuellin', Mrs Giddy.'

'That's true, Mr Farnham,'

'Anyways,' he replaces his cap and turns on his heel. 'Love to stay and chat but better get on. Loads more deliveries to make. Cheerio.'

'Cheerio, Mr Farnham. Have a good day.'

The doorbell tinkles again and the shop becomes still once more. Mr Farnham's van rattles and roars into life outside but quickly moves off and allows peace to return.

Mrs Giddy takes the eggs into the back and places them on the table in the centre of the room. Later, she will take six for herself - as usual - and divide the rest into half-dozen boxes.

She spikes the receipt on the shelf beside the door where the one from the milkman had been put earlier and where any others that she might receive during the day will be spiked too. She will attend to them all and the rest of the day's accounts before going upstairs later but now, she wants to get that cup of tea made before someone else interrupts her.

Some days, the interruptions are constant so that she doesn't enjoy a sip of hot tea from morning until night but Vera really doesn't mind. In fact she welcomes it. She loves not knowing who will appear over her threshold next and what news or conversation they might bring with them: so and so's child has just come down with chicken pox or the water board are digging up the road just outside the village again or the local cricket eleven did well at the weekend against Gorston Hatch. It is the unpredictability of her day that makes her life as a shopkeeper so interesting and, being the trunk of the grapevine (as she sees herself), there is rarely any news or gossip present in the community that she is not aware of. It is a situation she wouldn't want to change for the world.

Hence why the prospect of retirement gives such a bad taste. To suddenly have the daily flow of faces and gossip removed from her life will be like going deaf and blind. Taking away the thing she enjoys most will surely make retirement so dull.

Since Stan's passing, her evenings have been dull enough, sitting up there in her quiet little room in front of an uninteresting TV with a magazine or some knitting in her lap. If retirement is likely to be one long evening without Stan, well…she would rather keep the shop and continue working until she keels over.

Vera fills the kettle and switches it on to boil then rinses the old tea leaves from the pot. Yes, there was no way Stan would have been satisfied with a one-egg omelette. He may have been a wiry fellow but he could eat enough food for an entire regiment. She smiles at her use of one of his phrases then glances at the eggs on the table and wonders whether a two-egg omelette would have done him. She tells herself that, as large as they are, he would have accepted two but been happier with three.

Their plan had been to retire to the coast, Eastbourne or Hastings perhaps, and to get a tidy little bungalow somewhere within walking distance of the town centre and the seafront. They had first spoken of it years ago, shortly after getting married in '46 following Stan's return - mercifully all in one piece - from the terrible war in Europe. She had suggested it one day in an offhanded manner, more as a joke than a serious consideration but Stan had embraced the idea and so it had stuck with them and ingrained itself into their lives like a promise they had made to each other. As the seasons ebbed and flowed, the promise had matured into a plan, rarely mentioned and yet as firmly set as the bricks and mortar they would buy. Now that he has gone, taken from her far too early - as so many good people are - by cancer, the prospect of living the dreams they had shared, has lost much of its shine.

Yet Vera knows in her heart that the shop will have to go soon, if for no other reason than her own physical decline. She loathes admitting it but she is nowhere near as capable as she once was and with her rheumatism getting worse with each passing winter, the work is becoming harder and harder. There was always plenty to do even when Stan had been around but now there is much that doesn't get done at all. The shop, the flat upstairs, the little garden out the back, it is all looking a bit shabby these days and paying young Thomas Slaughter a bit of pocket money to do a few odd jobs on a Saturday morning or during the school holidays, well…the poor, young lad can only do so much.

However, the thought of leaving it all behind to start again, alone in a new home, fills her with apprehension. For a start, she is afraid that leaving the place where all of her happy memories have been made will only hasten them from her mind and, as daft as it sounds, she doesn't want to leave Stan, for she still feels his presence every now and again around the place and it gives her comfort. She doesn't think his presence will follow her if she moves away. On top of this, she can't help but feel that she is too old for a new start; all that organising and upset and hard work boxing up her life only to have to unpack it all again a little while later; what a nuisance!

Despite all her fears (and they seem to increase daily), Vera is the pragmatic type and she knows that change is inevitable if life is to continue. Her life will have to change again just as it did in '73 when she suddenly found herself a widow and, whether she likes it or not, she will just have to get used to it.

A plume of steam gushes from the kettle's spout and Vera switches it off. She pours the boiling water onto the fresh leaves in the pot, gives it a good stir and then covers it with a knitted cosy just as the doorbell tinkles again.

This time it is a young man she doesn't know, a painter judging by his spattered white-bibbed overall. He has narrow shoulders, an immature beard and a long fringe and she puts him to be about twenty-five.

Vera welcomes him before he reaches the counter. His eyes are dark brown and just a little too close together to look right. They give him a rodent-like appearance, which isn't helped by a thin, pointed nose and a weak chin. He glances at the cigarette shelf behind her.

'Yeah. Twenty B and H, love.' His tone isn't exactly friendly but it seems to match his general appearance. Vera suspects that he is frugal with his smiles.

'Is it still raining?' she asks, as she reaches for his order.

'Nah. Looks to be brightening up,' he says, peeling a note off a roll from his pocket. Vera takes his money and returns his change. 'Though that don't mean much,' he adds before thanking her and turning to go.

'You're right there. Have a good day,' she says, to his retreating back. The bell tinkles as he closes the door behind him and Vera wonders as she returns to the teapot if she will ever see his face again. Not that it really matters. Over the years she must have seen a thousand faces just once and well, some faces a thousand times. That's what life is like as a shopkeeper in a small village. Some people you know inside out, others are just passing strangers.

Vera takes a bottle of milk from the fridge and splashes a little into a cup. Then, tea strainer resting on the cup's rim, she lifts the teapot until a steaming gold stream curves out from the spout. She no sooner puts the pot down again than the doorbell tinkles once more.

This time, the shop is filled with the exasperated tones of a woman reprimanding someone. At first, Vera is startled but she soon understands what is going on. The bell tinkles again as the door closes but the raised voice continues it remonstration outside. Vera takes up her position behind the counter and waits. The door reopens and Mrs Becker, in trademark Barbour jacket and wellington boots, enters.

'Lord, give me strength,' she cries, as she strides forward. 'That dog will be mincemeat if it doesn't start behaving.'

'Problems?' asks Vera, with a sympathetic smile.

'Oh, Lord. You don't want to know. Good morning Mrs Giddy.' The tall woman with the educated accent dumps her straw shopping bag on the counter and huffs. Her equine face is flushed from her exertions. 'I cannot tell you how difficult this new dog of Adrian's is turning out to be. He's a devil on the lead and he will not sit still for two minutes.'

A bark comes from outside.

'See?' says Mrs Becker, brushing her harassed fringe from her eyes.

'Oh, that's right,' says Vera, remembering an earlier conversation the two had shared. 'It's that young rescue dog, is it?'

'Rescue? I think I need rescuing from him.'

Another bark comes from outside.

'Although if he doesn't shape up...' Mrs Becker leaves the sentence hanging. Whatever alternative she has in mind, she keeps to herself.

'I suppose that's the risk you take with rescue dogs, isn't it?' muses Vera. 'There's always a chance you'll have some problems with it.'

'Oh, good Lord, don't I know it,' says Mrs Becker, shaking her head. 'We've been lucky before but I don't know, maybe I'm just having a bad day and with...'

And quite uncharacteristically, Vera switches off. It has nothing to do with the fact that Mrs Becker is perfectly capable of having a long conversation on her own but today, Vera is in a pensive mood and her mind wanders again to the future she had imagined with Stan.

They had always seen themselves with a little dog in their retirement, a little companion to help keep them active with daily walks along the promenade and with their age likely to be a consideration, they had agreed that a mature rescue dog would be a wiser choice than a bouncing, peeing puppy. They had never been able to agree on the breed though for Stan had wanted a Scottish or Highland terrier whereas Vera has always liked poodles. Her parents had had one when she was a little girl; a lovely little white, bubbly thing called Daphne and young Vera had adored her. And as is often the case, the dog had reciprocated the affection and followed Vera everywhere it could. Now though, there will be no dog because there was no Stan and Vera can't help but look gloomily upon a future that will in all probability be a lonely one.

She is awaked from her reverie by the doorbell tinkling once more. Mrs Becker stops her nattering mid-sentence although what she was talking about Vera hasn't a clue. Charles Hurst enters, immaculately dressed as usual in blazer and half-Windsor knotted tie, his white moustache a perfect example of fastidious grooming. He stands tall and straight and moves as though he is on parade, albeit with a little less starch and urgency.

'Morning, morning,' he says, in a grunt-like manner to the women as he steps up behind Mrs Becker to wait his turn.

'So, Mrs Becker, what can I do for you today?' asks Vera, returning to her duties.

Mrs Becker rattles off a list of items she requires - a tin of this and a half pound of that and so forth plus an - oh, by the way, do you happen to have any of those? Vera is able to oblige her with everything expect the cherry red shoe cream she needs for the burgundy leather coat she has rescued from the back of her wardrobe and was hoping to spruce up in order to start wearing again. Then having paid and her straw bag full of weight, Mrs Becker opens the door and is greeted by a round of boisterous barking. She responds with equal volume although in a more wearisome tone than boisterous.

'Vera,' says Mr Hurst, stepping up to the counter and placing a strong, hirsute hand flat on its surface. 'A good morning to you.' His voice is deep and smooth and has always sounded to Vera like a big cat, perhaps a lion, purring - if, that is, lions purr.

'And to you, Charles. What can I do for you? Don't tell me you've eaten those humbugs already?'

Mr Hurst gives a snort of laughter and sways and bobs on the balls of his feet.

'No, no, nothing like that. That half pound will keep me going a good month, I'm sure. No, I was just wondering if um…you'd like to um…come and have lunch with me on Sunday.' His hard green eyes glitter like polished jade beneath thick but not unruly grey brows. Then as if he had left a bit off, he adds, 'Once you've finished here…' another pause, 'but of course, only if you've nothing else planned.'

The swaying and bobbing stops and for a moment he stands quite still, watching Vera's face. A hand flourishes up and fingers smooth his moustache. Vera wonders if she is seeing just a hint of embarrassment warming his cheeks but she can't be certain because his complexion is a little on the red side anyway, like his tie.

The invitation takes Vera quite by surprise and for a moment she is lost for words. Charles Hurst has been a good friend for longer than she would care to remember for he and his wife Gladys had arrived in the village soon after she and Stan had moved into the shop. Mrs Hurst's car accident three years ago had shocked the entire village and Vera had tried more than most to reach out and offer support to a fellow sufferer in those painful and disorienting weeks that followed the tragedy. Stan had always liked him as well.

Mr Hurst takes Vera's hesitation as uncertainty and follows up his invite with an explanation.

'It's just that,' the swaying and bobbing resumes, 'well, I rather enjoy a good old Sunday lunch but, to be honest I haven't had one in quite some time and yet…'

'Please, Charles, you don't need to explain. I know exactly how you feel.'

'Of course you do.'

'Unless my daughter comes for a visit, which isn't often, I don't bother with the Sunday lunch either,' admits Vera, her tone taking on a slight melancholy. 'It's only because I can't be bothered mind. It seems like such a to-do to go to all that fuss just for myself. But I love a good old Sunday lunch, as you put it.'

'You do?' His moustache stretches over a wide grin and his eyes shine with anticipation. 'That's splendid. So, what do you say then? You won't need to lift a finger. I promise you that. I'll take care of everything.'

The last time Vera had enjoyed a meal prepared by someone else was…well, it probably had happened but blessed if she can remember. The prospect is a lovely one.

'I would be delighted,' she says.

London's Alive!

The voice came over the PA system and announced Warwick Avenue as the next station. Typically, each overstated syllable was delivered as though we passengers were either dim-witted or partially deaf. I rose from my seat and pressed my way past shoulders and backs to the door as the tube train came to a smooth, whining stop. Rush hour had been and gone but there was still little room inside some of the carriages to swing a fast sideways glance, let alone a cat.

It was a little after 7p.m. and throughout the capital's network of subterranean arteries the giant electric worms continued their metallic gliding, ferrying London's lifeblood from organ to organ, point to point, station to station. It would be another six hours before the lines were dormant, albeit briefly, until the following day's cells were on the move again, nourishing, giving life to this metropolis that I call home.

It was with weary relief that I stepped out onto the platform amidst a score of other homeward bound commuters, just another piece of flotsam joining the flow. We funnelled onto the escalator as a surge of air, forced through the tunnel by another incoming train, pushed past us and raced on up ahead. For a few seconds hairstyles danced about like lambs in springtime.

I touched my Oyster card to the reader and the gate let me through. I headed for the steps and emerged a few moments later into a cool, still evening. Tree shadows and streetlights threw monochrome patterns across the ground and as I headed up the hill towards Little Venice and home, I dug my hands into the comfort of my coat pockets.

Hurried footsteps behind prompted me to step aside but as they drew closer, they slowed. I threw a glance over my shoulder. A man in a heavy coat and a baseball cap was just a few feet behind. Too close for comfort. I stopped and pulled my hands out ready to defend myself against this potential threat.

'Greg, it's me,' a voice said, the tone urgent but confidential. The man raised his cap a fraction, enough for me to recognise the face.

'Tully. Jesus! You scared me. What are you doing?'

'I need to talk to you but let's keep walking,' he said, grabbing my arm and urging me on.

'Why weren't you at work today?' I asked. 'Marion was annoyed you didn't call in.'

'Never mind that. Listen mate, I'm in trouble, big trouble and I don't know what to do.' Tully was an Aussie who'd made London his home several years ago. A handsome fair-haired man with coral reef eyes and a surfer's tan, he was normally the embodiment of laid back charm but right now I could see he was a bag of nerves. He was glancing this way and that like a pedestrian trying to cross a motorway. 'I hope to God you can help me.'

'I will if I can. What sort of trouble?'

'I'll explain everything but we've got go somewhere safe.'

The peak of his cap was pulled low again, too low to look right.

'What do you mean safe? What are you talking about?' I was too tired and hungry to play silly games and this seemed like a silly game. I stopped. 'Tully. It's been a long day. Just tell me what's wrong?'

Tully stopped several paces ahead. I noticed he was carrying a sports bag.

'Last night I saw something I wasn't meant to,' he said.

'Yeah, like what?' I wasn't up for guessing games either.

'Like the sort of thing you wouldn't believe.'

'Like what?'

'Like…I can't explain. Not here.' He sounded desperate. 'Come on, it's all here,' he urged, patting the bag. 'Shots you won't believe.'

The journalist in me immediately sat up straight. 'You mean you've got a story?'

'I've got something. I just don't know what,' he said.

We both worked for a small weekly freebie called, London's Alive! I put words in columns and he supplied photographs. We often worked together. Aside from a few snippets of mainstream news affecting the city and a spattering of celebrity gossip the primary aim of the magazine was to educate the capital's hip and trendy on where best to be seen and where not to be seen dead. Not exactly highbrow but it was a lot of fun.

'You don't know what? Tully, I don't understand,' I replied. My exhaustion was stretching my impatience to gossamer.

'Neither do I but please, Greg.' His vagueness was annoying but the promise of his photographs had me hooked. His paranoia seemed to infect me as well and I found myself glancing around with him, though for whom or what I hadn't the foggiest.

'You think you're being followed?' It was a stupid question to ask and the idea of it was utterly ludicrous but his manner was convincing. Either that or I was being a complete sucker.

'I don't know. I don't think so. I'm being too careful. But there's CCTV everywhere.' He pointed back down the road towards the tube station and shook his head.

'Hence the cap?' I queried, still unsure as to whether or not he was pulling my leg.

'I've got two other hats in this bag and I change them every now and again, just in case,' he said.

'Really? Mate, you've seen too many movies.'

Tully made no comment. I suggested we talk about his discovery at my place but he flatly refused to go there, apparently for my own good. Instead he suggested a bar - the busier the better - and so we turned and headed back down the hill to a pub I knew on the corner. I noticed that as we walked - and it was quite a hurried walk - he kept as much to the shadows as he could. Again, I wasn't convinced that he just wasn't being totally daft.

Despite being cool, the evening was dry and calm and the half dozen small round tables outside the Prince Regent were surrounded with people enjoying their drinks with a laugh and a smoke. We pressed our way through the crowd and went inside. Tully found a vacant table against a flock-papered wall while I ordered two pints from the bar.

When I sat down, I saw just how serious his face was. He looked tired and frightened, like a man who was petrified of his dreams. I took a sip of my beer but he left his alone. Beneath the low peak of his cap I could see his eyes surveying the faces around the room and every now and again they'd fly to the door as somebody else entered. It was quite unnerving.

'Do you have to do that?' I asked. 'I'm sure it's not that bad.'

He didn't respond; instead he continued his furtive surveillance.

'So, come on then. What have you got?' I asked, with a roll of my eyes. I was half excited, half dubious.

'This is big, Greg,' he said, leaning forward. 'I'm half sorry to be involving you but you're the only person I really trust.'

Another ludicrous admission. How could he say he only trusts me? Sure, we were pretty good friends as well as colleagues but I was quite certain he had numerous friends he was closer to.

'Yeah, yeah. Get on with it.' It all seemed a little melodramatic to me given that it was probably just a few photos of some celebrity cheating on his or her better half.

'Last night, I couldn't sleep so I went out with my camera…' he began.

'Yeah, yeah, like you do,' I added, aware that he often went out in the early hours with his camera when he couldn't sleep. In photography circles, he was quite well known for his shots of the sleeping city, a couple of which had won him national prizes and acclaim from his peers. Quite slowly but deliberately, he unzipped his bag.

'I was wandering around down by St James's Park,' his voice was low, 'when I heard arguing.' He pulled out, what at first glance looked like a deformed lump of black plastic. It was actually a Nikon SLR but there was a black cap where the lens would normally be, which was why it hadn't registered as a camera straightaway. He thumbed a few buttons on its back. 'It was a couple having a barny on a rooftop terrace along Birdcage Walk. It wouldn't have interested me if I hadn't seen who it was. Check it out.'

He passed the camera to me - keeping one eye on the room - and told me what to press to scroll through the photos. The first shot was dark and grainy but the next was better exposed and clearer. I recognised the man in it immediately. It was the Deputy Prime Minister. I lowered the camera to protect it from potential prying eyes.

'That's Hensley-Fairfax!' My voice was a harsh whisper.

'And that's not his wife, is it? Keep going. They get better.'

I brought up the next shot. The couple were both dressed formally, he in dark suit and tie, she in what looked like a very classy dress. A light source behind them - probably a patio light - coloured the edges of their silhouettes while the pale hue from the streetlights gave their skin a jaundiced pallor. The woman's hair was dark and wavy and she looked very beautiful but the photos, zoomed in tight as they were, captured her, as well as him, frozen in ugly moments of rage.

'Recognise her?' asked Tully.

'No,' I replied, flicking through several more shots. 'Should I?'

'She's the woman they fished out of the Thames this morning,' he whispered.

'Is she? My God!' Suddenly Tully's paranoia made sense. 'But how can you tell?'

'Keep going,' he urged, as if the woman's death was insignificant. The next frame had a big blue triangle in its centre, pointing sideways.

'You took a video, as well?'

'It got so interesting that I thought it'd be more useful. Press the play button and watch closely.' He looked nervously at a group of three men entering the bar but after a moment seemed satisfied that they were just in for the beer.

I bent over the camera in my lap and rested my forehead on the table. Anyone looking over might have thought I was having a nap. I pressed the play button and the scene on the terrace became animated. For a moment it disappeared from the screen as the camera strayed from its target but it returned in a beat and the couple continued their quarrel. I couldn't hear what the fight was about because the ambient noise in the pub was too loud but as I glanced up at him, Tully pre-empted my question.

'The sound isn't great. I was too far away. But I'm sure it could be enhanced in a lab,' he said, studying the faces of two more people entering.

I continued watching and the couple's arguing turned physical. First the man threatened her with a raised fist, then the woman lashed out. And then all hell broke loose as she went for his face with her nails.

'Jeez! They're going at it, now,' I said, aware of the sense of schadenfreude that had me smiling. 'Talk about being in the right place at the right time.'

'Has he hit her yet?' whispered Tully, across the table.

'No I don't...yes! Ouch!' I almost felt the blow as the woman went down. 'Jesus Christ Tully, this is gold. This'll be the end for the Deputy PM, that's for sure.'

Tully didn't respond.

The woman was no longer in the frame. Whether she had gone inside or was lying injured on the floor was impossible to tell but the video continued to play.

'Is that all?' I asked.

'Keep watching.'

'There's more?'

I kept watching. Hensley-Fairfax seemed to take a moment to compose himself. He leaned against the railing and looked out over the park, wiping a handkerchief across his face. His chest and shoulders rose as he took a deep breath and they sank again as he let it slowly out. He seemed to regain his equilibrium. Suddenly there was a flurry of movement behind him and his head took a direct blow from something. For a split second he seemed to grow in height, then he folded over the railing and fell out of the shot.

Shock made me utter something incomprehensible beneath the table. It must have been loud because Tully hissed a warning at me.

'But Tully, he just went over,' I said, as quietly as my excitement would allow. I looked up at my tired-eyed colleague and he raised his brow but didn't comment. Instead he insisted I keep watching. 'Tully, this is huge,' I whispered. 'You should've got this to Marion already.'

'Just keep watching,' said Tully. He seemed annoyed that I kept interrupting his video.

The screen became black for a second but then the lens zoomed out to a wider angle. It showed that the terrace was on the roof of a four-storey Georgian style building, which was fronted by grand colonnades supporting an impressive portico. Tall, narrow windows overlooking grounds that were surrounded by iron railings and hedges offered symmetry along the building's front and the one flank that was in shot. The walls were smooth and most probably painted white but in the electric hue of the streetlights, they appeared to be varying shades of eggshell.

The woman in the classy dress was a pinprick looking over the railing but as the camera zoomed in on her again, her distress was all over her face. She clearly realised that what she had done would have serious consequences.

Suddenly, Hensley-Fairfax appeared in the frame again and seemed to hop back over the railing as if it were only knee high from the ground. A look of utter astonishment came over the woman's face as the man stepped towards her and, grabbing her by the throat, lifted her up in one hand and threw her over the railing as though she were nothing but a handful of laundry. The camera zoomed out but was too slow to catch her falling. She had already gone.

My mouth hung open as though all intelligence had deserted me. A pool of saliva made its way out of the opening. Tully guessed which point of the performance I'd reached.

'Tell me that's not unbelievable,' he said.

'I don't understand,' I mumbled, blinking as though I too had just taken a blow to the head. 'He went over. He fell four, five storeys. He should...'

'Be dead? At least broken up a bit?'

'He must have landed on a ledge or grabbed on to something,' said my voice of reason. 'But I didn't...Here, how do I rewind it?'

'Let it go on,' said Tully. 'There's more. Anyway you saw the shot zoom out. You didn't see him hanging anywhere, did you? Besides, there wasn't anything for him to hang on to.'

'But that's impossible.'

'Is it? Don't you believe your eyes then?'

'But how could he not be hurt in such a fall? And how the hell could he get back up there so quickly?'

'He jumped, Greg. Didn't you see?'

'Don't be so bloody ridiculous. No one can jump that high.'

'Not humanly possible, is it?' Tully's tone and the expression on his face told me what he was thinking.

'Oh come on, Tully. You can't expect me to believe that.'

'No, you're right. I can't believe it myself. But I was there and that's what happened.'

'There must be some explanation. I mean it's just not possible.'

Another man looking vaguely familiar walked into the frame on the camera's small screen. He had silver hair cut short and a distinguished bearing and he peered over the railing next to the Deputy PM. 'Who's this, then?' I asked.

'You mean you don't recognise the commissioner of the Met Police? Sir Rawlins...' Tully clicked his thumb and middle finger as he tried to recall, 'oh, whatshisface.' A four-letter word flew from my lips. 'Haverstock! And any second you'll see the leader of the opposition join them,' added Tully.

And he was right. He did. All three men stood looking over the railing and they shook their heads in dismay and then glanced briefly out across the park. Haverstock exchanged a few words with Hensley-Fairfax and then they all retreated out of sight.

Stunned doesn't even begin to explain how I felt.

'God help us Tully,' I said, gravely. 'This is big. Scary big. Too big for the likes of us. I mean, who the hell else was up there?' But Tully didn't say anything. He just looked at me with anxious eyes.

'But there must be some explanation,' I said again, fumbling around in the cluttered corners of my imagination for a logical solution. 'Maybe they were filming a movie or something.' But it was such a pathetic attempt at reasoning that it didn't deserve a second thought. Tully simply shook his head.

'Trust me, I've been thinking about this all day,' he whispered, as he took the camera from me and put it back in the bag, 'and I've watched it over and again and the only thing that makes sense makes no sense at all.'

'So what are you saying? That our Deputy PM is superhuman or something? Or maybe he's a mutant like one of the X-Men?' My tone was cool and facetious and Tully's reaction was equally testy.

'I don't know, Greg. All I know is, I was there and now I have this,' he said, patting the sports bag beside him. 'And those people really aren't going to want me to share it with anyone, are they?'

'But he wouldn't have known you were there. Would he? He didn't see you.' It was a sensible presumption.

'He must have done,' said Tully, his voice heavy with foreboding. 'If you'd watched closely when the three of them were looking out across the park, you'd have seen Hensley-Fairfax look straight at the camera. It was only for a second but somehow he knew I was there, even though the trees hid me. Least I thought they did.'

'Are you sure? Did he come out looking for you?'

'I don't know. I panicked and took off.'

'Home?'

'I was going to go home but then...I don't know, mate. I just got paranoid and thought I was being followed. I mean, even though it was three in the morning and I was hardly the only person about...I just got a feeling, you know?'

I didn't know what to say.

The lines on Tully's brow exposed the weight of his fear. They were close-knitted like isobars on a windy weather map. His teeth nibbled nervously at his lips as he spoke. 'So, I went and hid out on the South Bank all night wondering what the hell I'm going to do. Just as well I did. This morning I called one of my flatmates - James, the one with the big ears - when I knew he'd be at work and he said two guys had come knocking for me at five a.m. They told him they were the police and insisted on looking around but he said they didn't show him any ID or give him any explanation. Just sort of barged in.'

'Was one of them Hensley-Fairfax?' I asked.

'I asked James if he recognised either of them. He said he didn't so I'm guessing not. They made a right mess of my room, apparently. Looking for the camera, I guess.'

'Why didn't you go to Clara's?'

'Why do you suppose, mate? I don't want to bring my girlfriend into this. Just in case, you know. Who can I trust Greg? I mean, you saw who was on that video.'

I shook my head in confounded sympathy.

'Who do you trust, Tully?'

'I trust you,' he said. 'But I don't know about anyone else. I really don't. Who do you trust?'

'With this? I don't know,' I sighed and spread my hands. 'It's so out of our league I can't even think straight.'

We both sat staring at the table as if it was about to turn into something magical and for a moment, the ambient noise level of the pub seemed to fade into silence as all my attention turned inwards and concentrated on the images that the video had seared into my memory. It was just incredible. Fantastic. Daft!

'Did anyone come to the office looking for me today?' asked Tully, after a minute.

His voice brought the surroundings back into my head but I had to ask him to repeat the question.

'Not that I saw,' I replied. 'Marion asked me if I knew where you were but she was the only one.'

'Would you trust her?' asked Tully. I thought about my answer before giving it.

'I think we have to. We can't just sit on this.'

I took a second sip of beer and encouraged Tully to do the same.

'I always said that lens of yours would get you into trouble one day.' I smiled and Tully managed to smile back. Then, an important thought occurred to me.

'You've made a copy, of course?'

'Yes,' he nodded. 'Haven't had a chance to do anything with it yet though. You want to keep it safe?'

'I won't keep it but I'll hide it somewhere for you, if you want.'

'Would you?' Keeping his hands out of sight, he pulled out his wallet and then slid a fist across the table towards me. I reached out as nonchalantly as I knew how and took the little USB flash drive from him and secured it in an inside pocket of my coat.

'So, how about we finish these then go and see Marion?' I suggested.

'You think we should?'

'We need to do something and the sooner the better,' I said. 'You'll feel better too, spreading the worry, so to speak.'

'I feel a little better already,' said Tully, smiling weakly again. 'Thanks mate.'

I raised my pint, inviting him to do the same, which he did. We didn't make a toast. We just drank deeply.

Ten minutes later, aside from a lacing of white froth inside them, our glasses were empty.

'Come on then, mate. Let's do it,' I said, rising from my chair. Tully got up and reached for his bag. He gave the bar another quick once over and came around the table.

'You don't want to go home first and tell Sal?' he asked.

'No, but I'll give her a call in a minute,' I said. 'She'll want to know why I'm not home for dinner. Just going to take a leak first.'

'Ok. I'll see you outside,' said Tully, adjusting his cap and moving towards the door.

While I was in the men's room, I slid into a cubicle and relocated the flash drive to my wallet, which I kept in the rear pocket of my trousers. It felt more secure there pressed tight against a buttock. I'd think about where to hide it properly later. Then I phoned home. Sal answered on the third ring. At the same time I heard somebody come into the toilet. Sal asked where I was. I heard the sound of a zip.

'Actually I'm in the gents down at the Prince Regent.' I kept my voice low. 'Listen babe, I'm sorry but something's just come up…I'm with Tully and, well, we need to go and see Marion right away.'

She sounded disappointed, just as I knew she would.

'I know but this is important,' I said. 'Really important.' The scratch of the zip came again from the other side of the cubicle door. It was followed by footsteps followed by the wafting of the door. Then silence. Sal described the meal she'd prepared for dinner; the image of it made my stomach grumble. I'd forgotten how hungry I was.

'I'm sorry. Maybe I can reheat it when I get in…I don't know. It might be late…I know.'

She urged me not to be too long then I hung up.

With my phone out I thought I might as well warn Marion of our imminent visit. I dialled her number. It rang.

And rang.

And rang.

Come on, Marion. Answer your damn phone!

She finally picked it up but just as I was about to launch into a plea for help, someone else entered the toilet. Then, I realised it was her voicemail that had answered the call but at the beep I felt I had to say something.

'Marion. It's me, Greg.' I was virtually whispering as I heard the person enter the cubicle next to me and lock the door. I looked up, half expecting to see a brutal face peer down at me but the tinkle of a belt buckle put me at ease. 'Listen, Tully and I have dug up something big but it's put us in a bit of a fix. We need to see you right away, so we're coming over.'

I'd been to Marion's place a couple of times before so I knew where it was. She lived in a large Victorian semi with rear views of Wandsworth Common. From her bedroom windows it looked like she had a back garden that went on forever.

There was every chance she wouldn't be home though because she was a woman with a busy social calendar but if she weren't there, we'd simply wait for her. She had to be shown this before she went to sleep tonight.

Together with the phone calls and then washing and drying my hands, it was seven maybe eight minutes before I stepped past the smoking throng at the tables outside. But I couldn't see Tully anywhere. I assumed his paranoia had persuaded him to stay out sight but after a few minutes of walking back and forth around the corner in the hope that he would spot me and emerge from his haven, concern began to gnaw at my nerves. I began calling out for him, quietly at first but then louder, my voice eventually reaching across the street to attract the attention of passers-by. But all I got by way of a response were some disapproving looks from the people outside the pub.

Concern quickly blossomed into dread, which began toying with my imagination the way a cat toys with a mouse it'd already caught. The chill of the evening was drawn to the sweat that had all of a sudden broken out beneath my shirt. One of the groups at the tables took an interest in me, their heads turning briefly in my direction and their conversations becoming muted and confidential, their eyes curious. Finally, one of them, a dark-haired twenty-something with patchy stubble spoiling a good-looking face came towards me with his pint glass held against his midriff and a swagger in his stride.

'You looking for that dude wearing a big coat and a baseball cap,' he said, his accent South African or Australian, I couldn't decide which.

'Yes. Do you know where he went?'

'No, man. But a couple a dudes got out of a van and chased him up there,' he said, pointing back up the hill towards the underground station. 'Looked like they meant business too.'

He started to say something else but I didn't wait around to hear it. I sprinted across the road in the direction he had indicated, cursing myself for having left Tully alone. It was a stupid, stupid thing to do.

I reached the tube station entrance in less than a minute and stopped, partly to listen out for anything that sounded like a scuffle, partly to catch my breath. In the four years I'd had this job, my fitness levels had plummeted significantly mainly because of the long hours and frequent boozy lunches. The best part of a pint of Fuller's London Pride sloshing about inside me didn't help much either.

I glanced this way and that, turning my head in the hope that my ears would pick up something of Tully, racing footsteps perhaps or a cry for help. Anything! But there was nothing; the avenue was a model of normality. Several cars drove by and a few people ambled past but there was no urgency or panic in their movements. They were simply on their way somewhere, home most likely. Tully, on the other hand, would probably be fleeing for his life and the energy required for that would stand out a mile.

I felt utterly helpless. I had no way of knowing where Tully was and therefore no way of helping him. He was on his own and I shuddered at the thought of what might happen to him.

Fear and confusion had a firm grip on me now. I just didn't know what to do. This was above and beyond any form of journalism I'd experienced. This wasn't interviewing an unwilling thespian or arguing with a muscle-bound doorman to let me pass or a maitre d' to re-check my reservation.

I did the only thing I could think of. I took out my phone and brought up Marion's number again. As the editor of London's Alive! and a lifelong journalist, she'd have a huge list of contacts and a better idea of how to handle this unbelievable situation. She was also a veteran of some serious events like the bombings and the riots so if anyone knew what to do, she would.

In my ear, the dialling tone seemed to be taking a long time coming so I checked my phone's display to see if I'd pushed the correct button.

It told me I had no service.

I felt the noose tightening. I'd made plenty of calls from here before, usually to Sal to let her know I was nearly home so I knew that I was not in a dead zone. No, this wasn't a network problem; this was something else. This was too much of a coincidence not to be.

My fear continued to swell like a rising floodwater and with it, the sense that my world was already under someone's microscope and getting smaller every minute. I felt like I was in a room where the walls were sliding in and that very soon, my attempts to hold them back would fail as I succumbed to the giant invisible forces behind them.

I just had to make that call.

I looked around for a phone box not knowing where one was; they're not something one tends to notice these days. But thank God, there was one right there behind the entrance leading down to the tube. I thanked God again when I saw it wasn't vandalised. Then I brought up Marion's number on my phone, dropped in a coin and dialled.

I heard the first three rings but not the forth. The door opened behind me and a gloved hand clamped over my mouth. An arm came around my neck and held me in an iron grip and as I struggled to free myself I became aware that the hand over my mouth smelled of a sweet spirit, which I knew wasn't booze. It tasted too peculiar on the back of my throat. My struggles became weaker; the hand over my mouth was sapping my strength and as I realised this, I was dragged forcefully backwards out of the phone box.

The sound of a car door slamming roused me. I had a feeling it was some time later. My head was throbbing like it never had before and my eyes felt like balls of hot lead burning in their sockets. Opening them hurt. I was in the passenger seat of a car and I reeked of whiskey or some such spirit. This time it was definitely booze but the taste in my mouth and the scratchy dryness in my throat were the remains of whatever had been on that glove. My sense of disorientation was overwhelming, probably similar to an avalanche survivor.

It was still dark outside, but really dark, as if I wasn't in the city anymore and the dashboard in front of me was a dim blur of colours. The car was running, moving slowly. I could feel the road gently massaging the suspension. I glanced over and through my cerebral pain and confusion I saw that Tully was driving. Only he wasn't. He was in the seat, his seatbelt was buckled but his head was hanging limply, chin on chest, jiggling ever so slightly with the movement of the car. His hands weren't on the wheel. In the gloom he looked as lifeless as I felt.

I tried to figure out what had happened but the blinding headache inside my skull bludgeoned any possible chance of reasoning and the physical torpor that crushed my strength prevented me from fighting it.

I felt the change in our direction though. We suddenly pitched forward and my head hung in gravity. The seat belt strained against my torso. There was near silence now as the road was no longer massaging the suspension. I had the feeling we were dropping but it might just have been me falling back into unconsciousness.

Living Without Wings

It was cool in the shade of the copse and through a gap in the trees Lottie Culpepper could see a pair of hawks wheeling effortlessly on thermals high above. They were gliding around an undefined centre with an almost hypnotic grace and for a moment she was completely absorbed with them. She was trying to imagine what it would be like to be up there, floating high above everything and everyone, to share their view of the multi-coloured patchwork of fields and woodland, of roofs and church spires, of roads and rivers. Just how far they could see? Could they see her house? Could they see the sea? Perhaps they could even see France. Lottie didn't know but she was sure that their view would be magnificent. Only God would have a better one.

It brought to mind her father and with him came the sensation that a balloon was being inflated inside her chest for she swelled with a mixture of awe and pride for him. She also felt a pang of envy because her father would know what the hawks saw because he was in the RAF and he flew aeroplanes. He would not have to imagine what the fields and forests, the streams and villages looked like from up there because he would have seen it for himself.

A loud splash drew her eyes to the pool below where she was sitting against the trunk of a tree. Her brother, Leslie, was thrashing about in the cloudy water attempting a rather clumsy backstroke and the sun filtering through the overhanging branches caught the spray from his energetic feet and scattered it with diamonds.

'Aren't you coming in then?' Leslie asked, as he caught her eye. He stopped splashing and lowered his feet to the riverbed where he began working his toes into the squidgy mud. At its deepest, the water came up to his chest but he bent his knees so that it covered him to the neck.

'No. It's too dirty.' Lottie wrinkled her nose as she shook her head and the fine blonde curls either side of her face brushed against her smooth, pink cheeks. 'And I bet it's not warm like you say it is.'

'Once you get in, it is. Why, I reckon it's almost as warm as a bath.'

'Oh Leslie. You're always saying things which aren't true.'

'Well, you won't know 'til you come in and find out. And it's only dirty 'cos I stirred up the bottom. Otherwise it's clean.'

Lottie frowned. She wanted to go in because it looked like a lot of fun but she was afraid. She wasn't a very good swimmer and the water looked too deep for her. She was only small, after all. Plus, despite what her big brother said, it was dirty. And she didn't for a minute believe it was as warm as a bath.

Lottie never could tell when her brother was teasing her. It seemed to be quite often and not at all dependent on his mood, which made it very difficult to know exactly when he was and when he wasn't. Leslie was three years older than she was and therefore, quite naturally, he knew a good deal more than she did about a lot of things. Lottie completely understood and accepted this fact because as her father was fond of repeating - 'the older you are the wiser you become', and wisdom in her mind was the sum of all you knew. You knew things by learning them and you learnt something new almost every day - something else her father had said on more than one occasion. She didn't have far to look for proof that this often-used phrase was true because her parents were clearly much wiser than Leslie and in turn, her grandparents were wiser still - at least, they looked it. This reasoning meant that she felt duty bound by a rudimentary law of the aging process to believe, or at the very least to consider, everything that Leslie said to her, even the fantastic-sounding and far-fetched things. That is, until she'd had time to digest and consider what he'd said. So even though she was fairly certain the river wasn't as warm as a bath, she couldn't be one hundred per cent sure until she checked.

Using an old length of rope that someone had once knotted to the trunk of a hornbeam tree, Leslie pulled himself out of the water on the opposite bank and stood on a narrow ledge looking across at Lottie. The bones of his immature body stood out like chalk fossils beneath his pale skin. He was naked except for his underpants, which were heavy and dripping with water and threatening to slip down but he didn't appear to be concerned by them. He took a backwards step then sprang forward and leapt as high as he could into the air hugging his knees and shouting - 'Geronimoooooo!' He landed with a great, noisy splash and disappeared briefly inside a bowl of erupting water.

Lottie slid out of the cradle of exposed tree roots she was sitting in and eased her way down towards the water, crawling spider-like on her hands and feet. She used the nubs and ropes of tree roots to steady herself as she went and the tip of her tongue betrayed her concentration.

When she was close enough to the water's edge, she reached a hand forward while her other hand held tightly onto a root behind her. Leslie, who had been watching her progress with wily interest, suddenly pushed his palm across the surface of the pool with all the force his shoulder could muster. The resulting fan of water reached right over his sister and sprayed her from head to foot.

It was so unexpected that Lottie was stunned. Horrified. The cold water took away her breath and for a second or two she froze like a statue. Leslie peeled away backwards like a seal, laughing with delight.

Lottie's shock quickly subsided and released her from its stony grip and as her breath came back she employed it by venting her outrage, squealing at her brother with fiery indignation.

'You rotter, Leslie Culpepper. You're such a meanie,' she cried, as she scrabbled back up the bank out of harm's way. She stood forlornly beside the cradle of tree roots and held her arms away from her body, as she looked herself over. 'Look what you done to my dress.' It was mostly her legs, her head and the arm that had been reaching forward that had got wet and water was dripping off her fingers and running down her legs into her sandals. It was also dripping from her springy curls down her face and onto the collar of her dress. 'Just you wait 'til we get home. I'm going to tell mum on you. Sometimes I really hate you.'

'Oh, Lottie,' said Leslie, still laughing. 'You're such a girl. Did you really think it's as warm as a bath?'

'No, of course I didn't,' said Lottie, pinching the cold, wet cotton away from her skin.

'Then why did you come down?'

'I wanted to feel how cold it is, that's why.'

'How warm it is, more like.'

'No. How cold it is. And it is cold. So I'm right and you're wrong.' She stuck her tongue out at him as if bringing the matter to a close with a full stop. Leslie laughed again, enjoying his sister's indignation. He stopped laughing though when he saw her scoop up his clothes and, giggling like a wayward pixie, run out of the copse.

'Oi! Come back here with my clothes, Lottie Culpepper. Lottie?'

August along the south coast had so far been a mixed bag on the sunshine front. Warm, clear days had been interspersed all too frequently with days of grey cloud; there had been cool spells and moments of drizzle and there had even been some early morning fog. Today though the sky was as clear and as unblemished as a freshly ironed bed sheet and the temperature was pushing eighty degrees.

Lottie ran into the field of chest high wheat that greeted her as she left the shade of the copse and trampled a path for about twenty yards before falling down breathlessly and giving in to her laughter. It was always a thrill to get one back on her big brother. She let go of his clothes and rolled onto her back.

The ears of wheat were still ripening in the advancing summer and the field, which was separated from its neighbours by busy hedgerows of hawthorn, blackberry and dog rose as well as isolated groves of ash, hazel and holly, was a gently swaying sea of feathery gold. But lower down the stalks were still green and cool and as Lottie rolled over and over, the tall stalks bent to her will.

Leslie climbed up the bank and emerged into the sunshine. He was dripping wet and the water met the hard earth at his feet and formed dark, dust-wrapped spots. He looked for his sister along the path that followed the river expecting to see her skipping the half-mile or so back to the village clutching his clothes. But she wasn't. She wasn't running in the other direction either. Then he saw the narrow trench of trodden wheat ahead of him and a devious smile crept onto his face. He slipped off his sagging underpants and gave them a good squeeze, wringing as much of the water out of them as he could, before pulling them back on. Then, with the sun fierce upon his shoulders, he tiptoed as quietly as he could into the wheat.

As he drew near the crater of flattened stalks that Lottie had made, she called out to him.

'I know you're there,' she said. 'I can hear you. So don't try scaring me.'

Leslie frowned with disappointment that his advance had been detected but even so, he rushed into the opening growling like a monster. Lottie didn't bat an eyelid. She was kneeling with her back to him and was watching a ladybird crawl through the fingers of the hand she held in front of her face. As Leslie approached her, the ladybird opened its tiny red shell, spread its wings and flew away.

'Oh, you frightened it,' she whined, as her sharp eyes lost track of its progress straight away. Leslie dropped to the ground and sprawled like a starfish in the sun.

'I feel all refreshed,' he gasped. 'You should've come in. It was smashing.'

'I didn't want to. You know I can't swim that good.'

'Yeah, but you got to practice to get better. Practice makes perfect, remember?'

'I know. But the water was cold and dirty. Anyway,' she said, as she sprawled herself out beside her brother, 'what are you going to do now?'

'I'm going to lie here a bit until I dry off.' Leslie wriggled his shoulder blades into the mattress of wheat until he was comfortable. 'Then...I don't know. What are you going to do?'

'I'm going to lie her until my dress dries off. Then...I don't know.'

Leslie smiled. Lottie watched her brother as he took a deep breath and then closed his eyes to the sky. She did the same. However, she found that instead of seeing nothing, her vision was filled with colour. She opened her eyes again and the bright orangey red became the pale blue of the sky. She blinked slowly several times - red, blue, red, blue. Then she covered her eyes with her palms. Black.

'What can you see?' she asked.

'I can't see anything. My eyes are closed.'

'So are mine but I can see red. Can you?'

'That's just the blood in your eyelids,' said Leslie.

'Is it really?' Lottie's eyes flashed in amazement but then she became suspicious that she was being teased again. 'Are you sure?'

'Sure I'm sure.' Leslie opened his eyes and turned his head towards her. 'Have you never held a torch to your fingers, like this, and seen all the blood inside?'

Lottie shook her head.

'It looks the same as your eyelids do now, only the sun's the torch.' Leslie settled again and closed his eyes. Lottie looked at her fingers. She held them up to the sky then brought them close to her eyes and then, not discovering anything of interest, laid them across her chest.

She remembered the hawks and looked for them but they were no longer around and she wondered if they'd got tired and landed somewhere. After all, as easy as they made it look, flying must be exhausting. I mean, walking wasn't hard work but no one would want to do that all day, she thought.

She was just about to tell Leslie, who seemed to have fallen asleep, that she was bored and that she wanted to do something when she noticed a swirling mess of white lines in the sky over towards the coast. Tiny black dots were scribing random patterns against the cloudless sky and although Lottie knew what they were - she'd heard lots of talk recently about the RAF trying to shoot down the German planes that had just started coming over - she'd never seen it happening. Suddenly she became excited.

'Leslie, look!' She sat up and pointed it out to him.

'What?' Leslie idly opened one eye, saw where she was pointing and then opened the other. He sat up with a jolt as though he'd woken from a bad dream.

'Wow! A dogfight. A dogfight, Lottie.' There was awe in his tone but then dismay. 'Oh, but it's too far away to see who's who.'

'Will Dad be up there?' Lottie was as wide-eyed as her brother.

'Oh, sis. How many times have I told you? Dad isn't a flyer. He's part of the ground crew.'

'Ground crew?'

'Yeah. His job is to get the planes ready for the pilots; refuel them like and make sure their guns are full of bullets. I wonder if they're our dad's lot. From Biggin Hill, I mean.' Leslie stood up and made a cowl around his face with his hands.

'So, Dad doesn't fly?'

'No, Lottie.'

Lottie remembered now that Leslie had told her before that their father wasn't a pilot. Her father had probably told her himself too but somehow her mind had always painted a rosier picture. She knew that the Germans were fighting for the skies over England - it'd been headline news for weeks - and somehow because of this, she'd always imagined her father to be one of those daredevil flying aces shouting, 'Tally-Ho!' like they do and then swooping up into the wide blue yonder to do battle with the enemy. It seemed a far more exciting and heroic vision than that of a crewman in overalls filling the planes with petrol. And she was positive that her father was a hero.

Leslie must have read the disappointment on his little sister's face because he turned to her and explained that their father's job was one of the most important in the whole RAF.

'Oh yeah, if the men on the ground don't get the planes ready for combat in double quick time,' he explained, 'the Jerries would be all over us. Why, they'd probably come right on over and drop their bombs wherever they liked blowing every airfield in the country to kingdom come. Then there'd be no stopping them. It's our dad and others like him that keep our pilots up there in the fight.'

'Really?'

'Really. Blimey Lottie, don't you know anything? And I heard Dad telling Mum when he was home last week how it's gotten really dangerous now that the Jerries are coming over and bombing the airfields. Why, it's my guess he has to run for his bunker two, maybe three times a day.'

Lottie smiled as her disappointment lifted. That sounded more like it, more exciting. Running from bombs, dashing into bunkers at the last minute before explosions shook the ground. That was heroic. She always knew her dad was a hero.

'I can't make out who's who,' said Leslie. 'They're too far away. But I just know our Spitfires are giving them Messerschmitts what for.' In his excitement, he made wings of his arms and started roaring around his sister, banking this way and that within the little circle of flattened wheat, roaring and swooping and stuttering like a machine gun. Lottie laughed with delight.

'Cor, I wish I was older, Lottie,' he said, when he stopped to catch his breath. A wistful yearning calmed his mood as he gazed up at the increasing number of contrails scarring the southern sky. 'If this war's still going on when I leave school, I'm gonna join the RAF. I'd give anything to be up there.'

'Do you think I could be a pilot too?' asked Lottie, her voice deadly earnest. It suddenly struck her how close her brother was to becoming a hero just like her father and well, she didn't want to be left behind. She could easily be a hero too. Leslie laughed but the expression on his sister's face persuaded him to temper his response with a little diplomacy.

'I'm not sure. You'll have to ask Dad if they let girls fly. I don't think they do. Anyway, come on. I'm dry enough now. Let's go home. This sun's making me right thirsty.' He pulled Lottie to her feet and then quickly got dressed.

The breeze was gentle against Lottie's face as she walked along beside her brother and it bore the sweet, dusty smell of the wheat. The air was filled with a thousand notes of a summer's day, the hedgerows being the choir stalls of the countryside where the birds sang out their hearts. There were choruses of finches and wrens, dunnocks and tits all gabbling like children in a playground and then there were the soloists, the blackbirds and the thrushes performing their splendid melodies for everyone to enjoy. The low drone of the honeybees added a soothing bass line.

Lottie and Leslie were talking about the cold lemonade they would enjoy at home when suddenly they heard the deep growl and stuttering *brrrpp* of an aircraft in trouble. They turned to see a single-seat fighter streak low over a dense thicket at the edge of the field maybe three hundred yards away. A line of dark grey smoke was streaming from just behind its propeller and even from where they stood they could see the holes ripped through the plane's fuselage and tail rudder. The white-outlined black cross of the Luftwaffe that stood out against the pale grey of its side loomed large in their minds like the presence of some terrible menace and as the children stood motionless, mouths agape, unsure of whether they should be excited or afraid, the plane swayed and pitched drunkenly as the pilot fought a losing battle with his unresponsive stick.

The engine choked and spluttered, then rose angrily on the throttle for a few seconds as the plane pulled up and over a looming bank of trees. The engine coughed once more and then died completely as the plane disappeared over a hedge and into the adjacent field. Lottie looked at her brother in the ensuing silence and he looked at her; they were both waiting for the sound of the crash.

And then it came. But it was more a series of thuds and the rattling and snapping of the plane's riveted parts than a big, deafening crash. Perhaps if they had been closer it might have been more dramatic but as it was, it didn't sound that bad.

There was one final thump as a solid weight hit the hard ground and then there was silence. Lottie was torn between wanting to investigate and wanting to flee to the sanctuary of her mother's arms. She'd heard that the Germans ate babies and while she was no longer a baby, she was the youngest here. If this German pilot were hungry enough, perhaps her six years and two months wouldn't mean a thing.

'Let's go and see if the Jerry's dead,' said Leslie, as he gave his sister's shoulder an encouraging shove. 'Come on.'

Lottie wasn't sure if that was a good idea but she didn't want to be left by herself so she ran after Leslie calling for him to slow down. The sound of her sandals slapping the hard ground filled her ears as she ran as fast as she could to try and catch up.

Leslie was waiting for her at the stile that connected the two fields. His chest was heaving from his efforts, as was Lottie's. He climbed up onto the stile and, balancing on the top rail, looked out across the field in the direction that the plane had gone down. Lottie glanced up at him and squinted as the sun blazed into her face.

'Can you see it?' she asked.

'Mostly. Looks like it's pretty broken up. It must have rolled over or something. Can't see the pilot though. Don't know if he's dead or not. Can't see the cockpit. Least it's not on fire.'

'What'll we do? Go back and tell someone?'

'No need, I doubt. I reckon someone else'll have seen it come down and would've already told Captain Fellows. The old fellas from the Home Guard will be here soon, I reckon.'

'Are we going to wait for them here?' Lottie's heart was still thumping hard against her ribs and it wasn't due to her sprint. She was exhilarated. Well and truly exhilarated. This was the most exciting thing that had happened in her whole life and she couldn't wait to tell someone about it.

'I reckon we ought to go and see where the pilot is,' said Leslie, climbing down off the stile. 'If he's alive we don't want him to escape.'

'But we won't be able to stop him. We're only little.' Lottie didn't really want to go near the pilot and she was hoping she could persuade her brother that it wasn't a good idea without sounding like a scaredy-cat.

'Yeah, but if he clears off, we can see where he goes, can't we? Maybe follow him if needs be. That way he won't give our boys the slip. We don't want him hiding out around the village getting up to all sorts, do we?'

'I don't know, Leslie. I'm a bit scared.'

'You'll be all right, sis. Just stay close to me. And if he wants to make trouble for us, well then we'll just have to run for it. Come on. Quietly now.'

Leslie took Lottie's hand and led her over the stile and along the edge of the adjacent field, which like the other was also planted with wheat. This crop had been sown a little earlier and so the wheat was taller and it seemed to whisper breathlessly at them as it swayed ever so gently in the breeze.

Unlike the field they had just come from which was dish-shaped with the copse and the pool being at its lowest point, this one had the contour of an upturned dish and rose several feet from its edges to a flat centre. It meant that from where she was, Lottie couldn't see the crashed plane; all she could see was a rising blanket of mature, golden wheat that cut a feathery line against the blue of the sky a short distance away.

'How much further?' she whispered, still holding Leslie's hand, which she noticed was as hot and clammy as her own. Leslie, who had assumed a stooping walk, lifted his head for a moment to take stock of their position. He quickly bent down again and his eyes were wide with excitement.

'It's just up there,' he whispered, pointing over his shoulder.

'Do we have to get any closer?' whispered Lottie, freeing her hand from her brother's and wiping it dry on her dress. 'I'm scared.'

Leslie pulled his lips into a tight line and frowned.

'Lottie. You're such a girl. Don't you want to see the pilot?'

She did, very much so, for all pilots were heroes, probably even the German ones but she couldn't shake the image that her mind had cultivated of the German soldiers gorging on piles of kicking, screaming babies. Ever since the war had started and the neighbourhood gossip and national airwaves had been full of talk about Germany and the German people, none of it had meant that much to Lottie. She'd never seen a German other than in a newspaper cartoon and was oblivious to the fact that she probably never would. But now, suddenly here, just a few feet away from her was one of the very people that the adults and older children in the village spoke of with such dread and loathing. Whether the stories were true or not, Lottie was more afraid now than she'd ever been in her young life.

'I don't want to be eaten,' she whispered. Her voice was so fragile that Leslie moved his head closer to her mouth.

'What?'

'I don't want to be eaten,' she repeated. Then with more conviction, 'Penny Wingate said that Matthew Carr's brother told him that the Germans eat babies. They pull their arms and legs off and eat them without even cooking them.'

'Blimey Lottie. Use your loaf.' Leslie rolled his eyes and his voice rose from a whisper as he straightened his back and shoulders. But Lottie's bottom lip began to wobble and so he softened his expression and continued in a gentler tone. 'That's just kid's talk. It's rubbish. I heard it too but it's not true. The Jerry's don't eat babies. No one does. Nor do they throw them in the air and catch them with their bayonets. People just say things like that to make you more scared of them, that's all. Blimey sis, you shouldn't believe everything you hear.'

And then he did something that surprised her. He reached out and tousled her hair the way her father does and the familiar gesture went a little way to untying the knot of fear that had grown large in her stomach. Even though he was but a mere three years her senior and less than a foot taller, the gesture gave her the sort of comfort provided by an adult; it was almost as though her father was there with them. Not quite, but almost.

'Honest?' The question was a plea, hoping above all else that he wasn't teasing her this time.

'Honest. Cross my heart.' Leslie made the sign that echoed his pledge. 'Now, do you want to wait here or do you want to come and see if he's dead or not?'

Before Lottie could say to her brother that, yes, she would come with him providing he held on to her hand all the time and promised not to let go, they heard something move in the wheat a little way off. The rustling stopped as Leslie raised his index finger to his lips. Trying to filter out the gentle swish of the wheat in the breeze, they listened intently for the sound again, but it didn't come. Perhaps they had been mistaken. Perhaps it was a mouse or something. Then, a dreadful, sickening groan full of pain and anguish came out the wheat. It caught Lottie's breath and took it away.

Suddenly the pilot of the aeroplane emerged out of the golden crop as though he'd risen from interment. He staggered to his feet and his heavy boots caught on the uneven ground as he lurched unsteadily towards them. His sweaty, oil-spattered face was a contortion of agony and a deep gash above his hairline was leaking blood onto his forehead, which pooled around his left eye and then ran down his cheek. A dark, wet patch on his tan flight suit covered most of his left thigh. Lottie screamed as he approached and Leslie's mouth fell open as he reached for his sister, pulling her to him as they clung to each other in terror. The instinct to run was shouting at them from all sides but in that instant, the ability to do so had abandoned them. The man reached out a bloodied hand and a gargling sound rose in his throat just as Leslie regained his wits. He pulled Lottie away with him and they ran back screaming towards the stile as behind them, the man tripped and fell heavily onto the bare earth at the edge of the field.

Fifty yards later, the children stopped running and turned their heads. Their eyes were wide and bright and their heartbeats were rapid and heavy. They stood and watched the figure on the ground. And they waited. If the birds and bees were still performing around her, Lottie couldn't hear them; all she could hear was her heart thumping the drums in her ears.

The seconds became minutes but the pilot remained motionless, sprawled on his front with his lips pressed against the dusty earth. There was no sign of breath left in him. His right eye - the unbloodied one - held the children in a vacant gaze and as they stood side by side and hand in hand, staring back at the lifeless face, they were both horrified and yet fascinated.

Across the field a voice carried on the breeze and pulled their attention back to their surroundings. It was joined by another voice and then another. Moments later, they heard people thrashing through the wheat calling out to each other, their voices familiar, their words for the plane and the pilot.

'That's Captain Fellows,' said Leslie, the tension in his throat relinquishing its grip on his vocal chords. 'Sounds like he's got the Home Guard with him too. Told you they'd be here, didn't I?' He jumped in the air and waved his hands high to draw them over. 'Over here!' He called. 'We're over here!'

'Who's that, then?' called a gruff voice that Lottie recognised as Mr Warriner's, the village bobby.

'It's me, Leslie Culpepper!'

'Leslie Culpepper? Young Leslie Culpepper? What the devil are you do over here?' The voices were all close now and they were all talking about the whereabouts of the German.

'He's not in the cockpit.'

'Probably got thrown out.'

'Look around for him, men. He can't be far. Be careful though. He might not feel like coming peaceful like.'

'If he's still alive.'

The stocky figure of Mr Warriner appeared above the children and came rattling down through the wheat towards them. His uniform was dusty from the field and with each stride, his tin helmet clonked against the canvas satchel that carried his gas mask. His heavy features made him look ponderous but his smile was a kindly one even though at the moment it was laced with concern. He greeted the children like an old uncle.

'Hello, you two. You oughtn't be here, you know?' he said, looking them over.

'But we saw it come down,' explained Leslie. 'We were over there,' he pointed behind them, 'and we came to make sure he wouldn't get away. That's all.'

'Is that right?' He knelt down in front of Lottie, pushed the rim of his police helmet up as far as its chinstrap would allow and gave her his warmest smile. 'Is that right, Lottie?' Lottie felt the embrace of his kindness and nodded. She was safe now.

'That's right, Mr Warriner,' she said, quietly. The policeman gave her nose a tweak and winked.

'Right you are, then,' he said.

'Better get them away, Bert,' said Captain Fellows, who had discovered the body of the pilot. His voice was cigars and whiskey and his formal, grey-haired bearing was a consequence of his military advancement during the Great War. 'Jerry's not going anywhere.' He pushed his foot against the inert body. 'Over here, men!'

Their mother was beating a rug that she had hung over the washing line when Leslie and Lottie, accompanied by Mr Warriner, opened the garden gate. She must have just started because with each *whump* of the carpet beater, a great cloud of brown dust jumped from the rug and drifted slowly across the garden.

The village policeman had told the children that he'd feel better if he escorted them home because they might be a little shocked by what they'd seen -

Lottie in particular. But by the time they'd reached the village, P.C. Albert Warriner had received an exact account of what they had seen as well as what they had been up to before the plane had appeared. He had laughed deeply and satisfyingly at Leslie's admission that his sister had run off leaving him with nothing but the underpants he was wearing but he had been less amused by their decision to approach the crashed plane before any grown ups were around.

'Supposing this Jerry fella weren't badly hurt and that he wanted to make a run for it,' said Mr Warriner, his voice still warm but quite serious. 'Supposing he were scared for his life and fired off his pistol at the first person he saw coming towards him. That might well have been one of you. Both of you, even. Do you realise that?'

Lottie didn't mention that they had thought of running away if the man wanted to make trouble for them; or at least Leslie had. It didn't seem worthwhile. Leslie kept quiet about it too, presumably for the same reason. But hearing Mr Warriner speak about the pistol brought it into sharper focus. Neither her nor her brother had thought about that. It had been silly of them and they had been lucky. But boy, what a story to tell everyone! She was nearly six and a quarter and she had now seen her first German. Not only that but she'd seen him die right there in front of her too.

Their mother stopped her rug beating when she saw the policeman enter the garden behind her children. She was wearing a light green headscarf and a pale blue pinafore over her summer dress but her feet were bare.

'What have you two been up to, now then?' she said, her tone light but reproachful.

Mr Warriner took charge of the explanation and began a much-shortened version of what Leslie and Lottie had told him but several times Mrs Culpepper had to shush her children from interrupting to allow him to continue. She was naturally relieved that they were unscathed, despite not having been aware they'd been in any danger but on learning that they had, she gave them the requisite scolding, albeit a lenient one. She followed this with the sort of reassuring hug that makes everything better.

When Mr Warriner had finished his report, Mrs Culpepper offered him a cup of tea but he turned it down on account that he had been halfway through his lunch when he'd been called to the plane crash. Now, he said, even though it was closer to teatime, he was going to run home and finish the other half. Their mother instructed Lottie and Leslie to thank him for walking them home after which he left with a smile and a wave.

Five minutes later, both children were sitting on the back doorstep guzzling their mother's homemade lemonade while she resumed her beating of the living room rug.

'I don't think I'll ever forget the way that man looked, sis,' said Leslie, his eyes unfocussed on a spot among the rose beds.

Lottie saw the German pilot in her mind's eye. She saw his bloodied face, as it lay cold and empty of spirit on the ground and a shiver ran through her.

'Nor me,' she said.

They finished their drinks in silence under the watchful eye of their mother who soon became satisfied that she'd beaten everything she could out of the rug. As Leslie got up to put his glass inside, Lottie reached for his arm. 'I'm glad our dad isn't a pilot,' she said.

Absurd Assignation

Roger Ballard forced a smile as his wife took her seat at the other end of the table. The muscles of his face assumed their positions with a willingness similar to that which one might display when pulling on an already sopping wet overcoat. But smile he did. After all, she was doing this because she loved him. Wasn't she?

'So, what delights do we have tonight, dear?' he asked, as he lowered his eyes to the plate in front of him.

Mavis picked up her napkin and smoothed it into her lap. Either she didn't register his tone or she chose to ignore it.

'That is a fillet of steamed haddock wrapped in a parcel of cabbage alongside cherry tomatoes and chives,' she said, with admirable enthusiasm. Her returning smile held more warmth than his but that wasn't difficult and her clear blue eyes searched his face for approval even though she knew she wouldn't find it. 'The carrots are steamed too but I tossed them in a little garlic oil just to wake them up a bit. There's less than two hundred and fifty calories on that plate.'

'Huh. Who'd have thought? And these green bits?'

'Chives, dear.'

Roger clenched his teeth. He didn't know much about calorific values and such like but he was pretty sure that two hundred and fifty wouldn't even provide the energy needed for his daily fingernail growth.

He looked up from his plate and regarded his wife with a scowl that he knew shouldn't be there and for a moment, he found himself harbouring an urge to attack her with a barrage of unjust criticisms. But he didn't because Roger wasn't that way. He didn't have an unkind bone in his body - not really - and so the urge quickly abated. This new diet was just making him feel grumpy, that's all.

He sighed and tried to relax. After all, from now on, this was the situation and he had to get used to it. He scrutinized his wife's face at the end of the table, her hands and her clothes as she began to undress her little fish parcel. She was still a neat little thing, he'd give her that; a little priggish perhaps and somewhat old fashioned but possessing the right balance of pride and vanity so as to be a decent, self-respecting person but not so much as to be self-absorbed or arrogant. She didn't have a great sense of humour but then neither did he. She wasn't what he'd class as fun to be around anymore either, but then he didn't suppose he was either. But she was a steadfast companion, reliable, sensible and as loyal as a gun dog.

In many ways she looked to him remarkably similar to when they had first met in that far off summer of '68 - God, was it really that long ago - when fate had conspired that they share a car together on the Wild Mouse ride on Blackpool's pleasure beach. The way she had screamed with the thrill of the fast turns and the heart-in-the-mouth dips and then blushed her shame when it came to a stop because she was gripping his hand as if it was her only lifeline…well, it had enchanted him. He used to tell the story that they saw each other frequently over the remainder of that holiday and that when they went their separate ways they had promised to keep in touch and to see each other again one day. And they did four months later at Christmas during which they admitted their feelings for each other. But the truth was, Roger had fallen for her even before the Wild Mouse ride had ended. Fortunately for him, she had done likewise.

Naturally, she was a little heavier now but she still had that pleasant and kindly face that had bewitched him all those years ago. The lines of time were barely evident on her cherubic complexion but then, with her twice-daily applications of scrubs, balms and creams, that was no great surprise to Roger. She seemed to take greater care of her face than anything else he could think of and he often joked about calling the Oil of Ulay people or whatever she used nowadays because she was a perfect walking advert for their product.

The most obvious change in her appearance was her neck. Once long and slender it had endowed her with an Audrey Hepburn-like poise but over the years it had thickened and integrated with her shoulders the way the roots of an old tree reach out above the ground. But at least she hadn't developed a double chin, as he had. In comparison to his wife, Roger knew he had let himself go - with both hands.

'So, no roast potatoes then?' he asked, picking up his knife and fork. It was only a joke and he knew Mavis would know that but he thought he'd ask anyway. Actually it was more of a dig than a joke but he couldn't help himself. At that moment there was a greater probability that the Duke of Edinburgh would pull up outside on a primrose yellow Vespa and ask if he could sleep the night on the sofa than there was of being some beautifully crisp on the outside and fluffy on the inside roast potatoes in the house.

Roger sighed again.

Mavis cocked her head and smiled demurely at him.

'You know there isn't, dear,' she said. 'And we won't be combining our proteins and carbohydrates for a while yet. And even when we do, we'll be wise to only do it on occasion.' She popped a polite morsel of fish into her mouth.

'You mean like mealtimes?'

Mavis's shoulders dropped a fraction at her husband's remark as though she was an inflatable and had suddenly lost a few pounds of pressure. Her eyes fell sideways in a barely noticeable roll. She waited until she had swallowed her mouthful before responding.

'Oh, come now, darling. It's not that bad. It's only hard at the moment because we're breaking the habits of a lifetime. We've been eating badly far too long and if it wasn't for that medical you took for the insurance company, the doctor wouldn't have discovered your little problem and you'd still be eating yourself into an early grave, wouldn't you?'

Roger frowned at the way she called his recently diagnosed angina 'your little problem' as if it was uniquely his. He suddenly wished he existed in a Jules Verne universe where he could jump on his time machine and go back to the moment before he had the idea of reviewing his pension. After all, this whole thing was his fault. A shrewd moment of fiscal thinking had turned into a waking nightmare for him and Roger was sorely tempted to just come out and admit that he'd rather die soon and sated than suffer even just one more intolerable meal like this.

Yes, he understood that his wife's intentions were sound and that as always, she was looking at the big picture rather than living each day as it comes, as was his habit. But as far as he could see, it was one thing to keel over and be gone in a moment of heart stopping agony but another thing entirely for one's light to almost extinguish and consequently render them a burden to their nearest and dearest for weeks, months, or even years. This was the scenario that Roger feared more than anything else, the idea of being infirm. Surely that was a fate worse than death.

'Perish the thought,' he said, as he slid his knife across the corner of the cabbage parcel and tried to conceal a grimace as a pool of tomato water bled across the half empty plate.

'Don't forget dear, it was your results that persuaded me to get checked too. We'll both be in trouble if we don't make these important changes stick.' Mavis seemed to relish the thought that they were in the same boat. 'Anyway, even after just two weeks,' she continued forcing home the positive, 'it's clear we've both got more energy. Why usually, we'd finish our dinner and flop in front of the telly and do nothing until bedtime. Now we're both up and out doing all sorts of things, using our time instead of wasting it. Doesn't that make you feel better?'

'Indeed,' agreed Roger, trying to swallow a mouthful that didn't want to go down. 'I never knew how much I enjoyed the garden,' he said, with an airy nod. 'Which reminds me; tonight I must pop back to B&Q and see if they've got the bags of special chippings I ordered the other evening.'

'You see. Not only are you taking up a new hobby, but you're getting good, healthy exercise too. Why soon you'll be as slim as you were when I met you.' She smiled sweetly again and Roger felt a pang of yearning for days gone by - and not decades ago either but just last month when meal times were something to look forward to.

'Uh huh.' He worked his teeth through a forkful of garlicky carrots.

'And I've never been busier,' offered Mavis, pressing her napkin to the corners of her mouth. 'I'm popping over the road after dinner to chat with Sandra about our next book for our reading group. It's my turn to choose.'

'Good Lord,' mumbled Roger, almost to himself but not quite. 'Things are so different here now, when the kids visit they won't recognise us.'

With such scant servings, mealtimes for the Ballards were now short affairs. No more did they linger over second helpings or open new lines of conversation over desserts as they slowly sipped that second glass of wine. Now, the only drink on the table was water and the single, unexciting serving of food was ingested as quickly as was politely possible so that the newly discovered interests could be indulged and the unremarkable fare forgotten. It seemed as though the dining table, which had up until a short time ago been a hub of relaxation and fulfilment for them both, had become a place to spend as little time as possible, like an unlit car park in a dodgy part of town. Less than forty-five minutes had elapsed between the moment Roger had sat down at the dining table and his turning the key in the ignition to start the car.

'Please, none of this "sir" business,' said Roger, to the landlord of the White Hart a short time later. 'If I'm going to be coming in here regularly then I insist you call me Roger.' He slapped the top of the bar with his hand as if he was passing a new law.

'Fair enough. Roger it is,' said the bearded, pot bellied landlord. 'And I insist you call me Peter.'

'Will do, Peter.' This was the fifth time Roger that had been in the pub in as many days but it was the first time he'd actually taken the time to chat with the landlord.

'So Roger, will you be wanting to look over the menu again this evening?'

'No, I don't think so. Just bring me a large glass of your house merlot and a steak sandwich with chips, please. I'll take a seat through there.' Roger pointed towards the dining area.

'One large merlot and a steak sandwich with chips coming up.'

The evening was still young and most of the brushed red velvet chairs arranged throughout the spacious bar were vacant. A CD player behind the bar span out an '80s pop song, the upbeat melody coming out low and unobtrusively through the network of speakers fixed discreetly at various points around the bar's dark wooden beam work.

Roger was aware of the absurdity of what he was doing as he pulled out a chair and sat down but he couldn't help himself. Somewhere in the back of his mind he felt a vague connection with a drug addict desperate for a fix and an unfaithful husband meeting a lover. What he was doing was wrong but it was something he felt unable to avoid. He knew that if he'd gone to bed with nothing other than the dinner

Mavis had prepared, he wouldn't have been able to sleep. His empty stomach would have rumbled like a central heating system plagued with air pockets and his hunger pangs would have had him writhing about beneath the duvet like a landed tuna on a wet deck.

He took no pleasure in his betrayal, at least not in the act of committing it. He got immense pleasure from it. He was well aware that Mavis was making these changes for his benefit more than hers and that she was probably suffering just as much as he was. The doctor had advised her that she'd do well to eat a healthier diet but the truth was, she hadn't been put on medication for the rest of her life and so she obviously wasn't in the danger zone as was he. The changes were, for her, a mere suggestion, a show of support but for him they were a necessity. She'd be terribly disappointed and quite likely very annoyed if she found out he'd been appeasing his appetite in a nearby pub like a junky in an alley every evening he went out with some flimsy excuse about fetching something from the garden centre or taking the car to the jet wash.

A young woman with ironed straight hair and a black skirt that enwrapped her comely shape like a tube of surgical bandage toddled over and furnished the table with the glass of merlot and a wire basket containing cutlery and condiments. Roger eyed the rich burgundy liquid in the glass with the desire of a cat eyeing a bird in a cage. His tongue moved slowly between his lips but he resisted the urge to swig it down before his food had arrived. He'd only want a second glass. He took a sip but only a sip and a little over ten minutes later the waitress returned with his food.

'Enjoy your meal,' she said, before toddling away again.

Roger gathered his cutlery but took a moment before diving in; he wanted to make the moment last as long as he possibly could; he wanted to devour the meal with his eyes and his nose, to arouse his taste buds until they were begging for deliverance.

The chips were golden and crispy, the steak between the fresh crusty baguette was seared dark and dripping with meaty juices, there was even a salad garnish to lend the plate a little bloom of colour. Tendrils of steam rose into his face and with them came the intoxicating aromas of seared beef and potatoes deep-fried in oil. This highly anticipated sensory event produced a major chemical explosion inside him and the sudden release of enzymes and gastric fluids surging through him bore unto Roger an overwhelming sense of gratitude simply to be alive. If he were a praying man he would have got down on his knees right there and then.

He began with another sip of wine. The merlot wasn't the best, but it was smooth on his tongue and warm as it went down, and after he'd swallowed, it left a soft impression of black cherry on his palate.

Mavis Ballard was sitting at the kitchen table beside her neighbour Sandra Carville. They were sipping gin and tonics while leafing idly through a selection of home décor magazines. A blank piece of paper and a pencil sat beside Sandra's elbow. A mere six years separated the two women but to see them side-by-side, you'd think it was a generation. Where Mavis dressed in three quarter length skirts and collared blouses, Sandra wore denim jeans and T-shirts. Mavis had an outdated - albeit tidy - shoulder length hairstyle whereas Sandra's was cropped and sat somewhere between scruffy and cool. Years ago, Mavis had found a look she was comfortable with and as it wasn't broken, she wasn't going to fix it. Sandra on the other hand continued to find her way, chameleon-like, through the ever-changing fashions of the times.

'What about that one?' Sandra asked, pointing to a picture of a large chesterfield style sofa in her magazine.

Mavis wrinkled her nose and made a whining sound.

'No, you're right. It's ghastly.' Sandra turned the page quickly. 'My God! This shouldn't be so hard. It's just a sofa.'

'But they're expensive and you want to get one you like.' Mavis was turning pages without really seeing what was on them.

'Maybe I'll just go to IKEA. What do you think? IKEA?'

'It wouldn't hurt to look. Do you think the group would like to read a classic?' asked Mavis, returning to the reason for her visit. She said it whilst eyeing the slices of tomato and mozzarella bruschetta Sandra had made as an appetiser. 'I can't tell you how hard I'm resisting those.'

'Oh well, what he doesn't know won't hurt him, as they say,' said Sandra, with a smile. 'And I won't tell. Go on, help yourself.' She closed the magazine with a huff of frustration and opened another.

'I'd love to but I can't. Really I can't. Having this drink feels like a sin too far. Roger's suffering, I know he is, so I'll suffer with him.'

'Wow! You're a good wife, Mavis. I'm not sure I'd be so steadfast.'

'Really?' Mavis seemed surprised by the admission.

'Well, I don't know. Hard to tell without actually being there. But back to your question - I don't see why the group wouldn't like a classic. We've read them before though not for a while. Who are you thinking of - Hardy or Austen, someone like that?'

'As much as I love her, Jane Austen is a bit obvious, isn't she? Anyone who reads has read Austen but Hardy - now he might be more interesting. I've only read Tess of the d'Urbervilles but that was a long, long time ago. Do you think everyone else would agree?'

'It's your choice, Mavis,' said Sandra, scribbling down the name Hardy on the paper. 'As the group's newcomer, you get to choose the next book. That's the rule. And it can be anything you like. It can be The Hungry Caterpillar if you want. For my mind, Hardy would be a nice change. I'm getting a bit sick of international crime thrillers and quasi-erotic romances.'

Mavis hummed thoughtfully and then drained the last of her G and T. Her lips made a sucking sound against the ice cubes.

'You want another?'

'I shouldn't but…well, I'm being naughty anyway so, why not! Though, please don't let me get tiddly.' Mavis passed Sandra her glass. 'He'll be upset if he finds out.'

'Oh, the little white lies we have to tell them, eh?' Sandra moved to the fridge to recharge their glasses. 'So you're really just doing this to support him, eh? That whole thing about the doctor advising you to change the way you eat as well is all made up?' As she spoke, she deftly splashed two fingers of Gordon's over fresh ice then added slices of lime and a generous measure of tonic into each glass.

'Yes. All made up, I'm afraid. I knew it was the only way to get him to change his habits. Bless him. He's probably doing it just as much for me as he is for himself.' Sandra handed Mavis her refill. 'Thanks. Sometimes you just have to tell them what you think they should hear.'

'Cheers.' Sandra raised her glass. 'I can't tell you how often I've told Stephen things that aren't strictly true just to get him to do something or to keep him sweet.'

'It gets so that it becomes habitual, doesn't it?' said Mavis. 'Still, there's a point to it, I suppose. It's getting him off his backside in the evenings.'

'And that's a good thing, isn't it? So in my book your little deception - if I may call it that - is completely justified.'

'It's for his own good,' said Mavis, with virtuous simplicity. She raised her glass towards Sandra.

'To his good health,' said Sandra, bringing the glasses gently together.

Roger's second meal took slightly less time to put away than his first but unlike the earlier plate, this one was devoured instead of suffered. Every mouthful of juicy, fatty steak, every bite of every crisp, yet fluffy chip had his taste buds singing 'hallelujah!' Midway through the meal, he even let out a burst of laughter as he realised the irony of the thought that came to him - this plate of hearty fare was exactly what the doctor ordered.

When he had finished, he emitted a deep gratifying hum as he leaned back in his chair and lovingly caressed the swell of his belly. And savouring every drop, he drank off the remainder of his wine. He was now a very contented man.

He paid the bill - in cash, naturally - and then drove to B&Q. He hadn't actually placed an order for some special chippings; it was merely the first thing that had come to mind at the table but he decided to follow up the idea all the same. Laying something like Cotswold Chippings on the path that ran down the side of the house was a possibility that had been in his mind for a while.

He looked at various grades of chippings and decorative stones just to get an idea and took a brochure as proof he had been there. It probably wouldn't be needed but it was better to be safe than sorry. How childish, he thought; a man of his age resorting to cunning and deceit like a teenager smoking behind his parents' backs.

Browsing through the gardening section, he bought some slug pellets to protect the new dahlias he'd planted at the weekend as well as some more weed killer. At the checkout, he also picked up a tube of mints. He'd quickly assumed the habit of masking any lingering oral whiff of his betrayal on the way home from the pub.

Mavis was still over at Sandra's when he pulled into the drive. He scattered some of the slug pellets around the garden and knocked about in the shed for a few minutes, the main purpose being to get an idea of what else he could pick up from B&Q on his next visit. It was just after 9 o'clock when he went inside and finally flopped down in front of the TV.

Mavis returned around half an hour later. To Roger's question, she replied that she was happy to have decided on which book to choose for her group - The Mayor of Casterbridge by Thomas Hardy, however Roger thought she seemed embarrassed by her choice as though the other girls in the group wouldn't like it for she was fidgety and her cheeks were flushed.

'I'm sure they'll be fine with it,' said Roger, interpreting her expression as worry. He didn't know what the book was about and so he had no opinion but he was still sure they'd like it. Mavis didn't respond. Instead, while she remained standing by the door, she asked about his evening and he told her in as little detail as possible that the aggregate he had ordered from B&Q was no longer available and that he'd have to select a different one from the brochure he had been given. The little white lie appeared to satisfy her because all she said was that she was sure he'd choose the best thing for the job. Then with a furtive little yawn, she went upstairs to have a bath leaving Roger patting his stomach in peace.

'Roger, dear?' Mavis turned her head on the pillow. The lights had been out only a few minutes but long enough for her eyes to adjust to the gloom. She could just make out her husband's profile.

'Hmm?' Roger's eyes remained closed and his chest rose and fell silently. He was drifting already.

'You are taking this diet seriously, aren't you?'

The question pulled him rudely back from the precipice of sleep. Did she suspect? How could she? Or was he being completely naïve? Roger forced himself to not react in a way that might convey guilt.

He was new to this lying business and probably far from adept. He willed his voice to remain low and calm.

'Why do you ask?'

'Oh…' There was a long pause and Roger opened his eyes. He felt certain she was about to denounce him. 'I suppose I can't bear the thought of losing you,' she said quietly, 'that's all. Silly really.'

'We've all got to go sometime, my dear.'

'I know that. But promise me you'll do your best to stick with it.'

'I can't say I like it but I know we've got to do it if we want to stay out of trouble,' said Roger, the ambiguity of his reply making it easy to say.

'I know it's hard but please…promise me you'll do your best. That's all I ask. Just your best.'

Roger was reluctant to make such a pledge but he knew that to not do so would be as good as telling his wife he didn't care about her. He had to mirror her show of support. Really, he just had to. It was like an entente cordiale. He thought about his response and of the consequences and the seconds of silence stretched on until it rattled him. Finally, after a deep, silent breath he took the plunge.

'Of course I will, dear.' He wanted to add that he was doing it more to support her than for his own good but he thought that would only invite a string of protests and as he wanted to go to sleep he left it unsaid.

The pillow rustled again as Mavis turned her head away.

'Thank you.' Her voice was a wafer but he heard it.

After a while, his wife's breathing became deep and rhythmic and he knew she had gone to sleep satisfied.

He, on the other hand, stared blankly up into the gloom for nearly two hours before sleep came for him. In that time, he thought of nothing but the meal he had enjoyed earlier that evening and he recalled over and again every sight and every smell and every taste. But for Mavis's sake, it would have to be the last time he had a bit on the side.

Later in his dreams he saw the same steak sandwich and chips sitting deliciously in front of him at the White Hart. He was as naked as the day he was born but that didn't seem to concern him. As he reached for his knife and fork to appease his craving hunger, his doctor called out to him from behind his desk, waved a finger of caution, and then he got up and walked over and took the food away. And in his dream Roger cried like a baby.

Beast of Burden

The mid-morning sun fought through the grime on the window and cast a shaft of yellow light across the cool, quiet interior of the little shed. Myriad specks of dust became visible as they entered the beam and for a few moments floated serenely through it before disappearing again into the musty shade.

The silence was broken by a series of hammer clouts as Sam nailed the rear axle to the go-kart he was making. He had come up with the idea a few days ago and after sketching a simple design, he'd hunted through the crusty corners of his father's old shed with his best friend Jason and found the necessary scraps of wood to make the frame.

It was as basic a go-kart as one could make but that was exactly what Sam wanted. Nothing elaborate or unnecessary, just a simple, light kart that could easily be dragged or carried back up whichever hill they had just sped down. His vision was little more than a carpeted board to sit on, about the size of a fridge door, a length of wood screwed centrally to its underside and, connecting in a 'T' via a hefty bolt, a foot rest that doubled as a steering bar. Axles fore and aft, a length of rope to hold onto and aid steering and there you have it - the perfect, lightweight downhill racer.

Every weekend, the council brought a big yellow skip to the village for the locals to fill with any rubbish that was too large for their dustbins and that skip was like an X on a treasure map for any young lad taking on a project such as go-kart building. Earlier that morning, amidst the grass cuttings and battered remnants of old furniture, Sam had unearthed a broken pram with four wheels that were perfect for his needs. He stood back and admired his handiwork. If Jason was having any luck sourcing the other bits, the kart would be ready to use in no time.

He'd barely finished that thought when the shed door opened with an apologetic squeak and Jason's mop of curly blond hair appeared. He lived next door to Sam and they had become solid friends soon after their mothers had enjoyed their first neighbourly coffee together almost six years ago.

Jason was tall for his age and already had the broad shoulders of a young man and because of this, he looked several years older than Sam. By nature, he was fearless and impulsive which often led to the first aid kit having to be fetched or worse, a trip to the hospital. This aspect of his friend scared Sam a little, who was far more careful and methodical, and preferred to plod instead of rush. However, Sam was often glad to have such a big, strong ally. Likewise, Jason was constantly amazed by Sam's ability to figure things out in his head and to come up with ideas and snippets of information that were, for the most part, interesting and useful. If he ever got stuck on something that required brainpower, Sam was usually obliging with the answer.

'Hey Sam, how's it going?' Even Jason's voice sounded grown up compared to Sam's.

'I've got the back wheels fixed,' replied Sam, a proud grin of achievement lighting his face.

'Well, take 'em off again,' exclaimed Jason, with great self-importance. 'I've got something better.'

'What do you mean?' asked Sam. He looked at his friend with a mixture of suspicion and concern. From behind the door Jason produced a wheelchair that he said he'd just found in the skip. He'd gone there looking for a scrap of carpet for the seat but found a large pair of wheels instead.

'They're filled with air too so they'll make it more comfy,' he explained. 'And they're bigger which means they'll be faster.' Jason's face radiated enthusiasm like he was on a TV advert for some must-have product. 'And that's not all,' he went on. 'Remember what my brother said yesterday about the seat? Well, ta da!' He flung the door wide open to reveal a wheelbarrow in which sat a front seat from an old mini.

Jason's older brother, Guy, had breezed into the shed the day before to see how things were progressing - cheese sandwich in one hand, mug of tea in the other - and convinced Jason that a proper car seat would be far and away a better place to sit while hurtling down nearby hills. 'You wanna be cushioned from all the lumps and bumps in the road, don't ya?' he'd suggested before leaving them to it. This had sent Jason on a feverish hunt for just such an item and with a little ferrying around from his mother the nearby scrap yard had come up trumps. Sam glanced across at his sketch on the workbench.

'But...' he began.

'No buts Sam, this'll make it the best go-kart ever! Now give us a hand, will you?'

The two boys carried the car seat into the shed and after a bit of careful measuring and marking by Sam they lifted it into place. Then, with the dexterity of Thor, Jason hammered the brackets down to secure the seat to the base of the kart. He wiped a grubby forearm across his brow and his amber brown eyes shone like polished brass buttons.

'Will you look at that,' he said, in a tone that was the verbal equivalent of a pat on the back. 'Whaddya think?'

Sam could see only its failings and with a shake of his head he said, 'But it's made the whole thing so heavy. Do you know how hard it's gonna be to drag up hill? And we'll never be able to carry it.' He matched his actions to his words and lifted the rear end of the kart. While it wasn't impossible, it was a bit of a strain and he frowned at the thought that Jason was getting carried away and deviating unnecessarily from his original drawing. A light kart was an easy one to move when you weren't going down hill and Sam was farsighted enough to know that they wouldn't be going down hill all the time.

'Yeah, but the heavier it is, the faster it'll be. That's what physics are all about, I think,' countered Jason. 'Now then, whaddya reckon about a pair of mirrors. I know where we can get some.'

'Mirrors?'

'Course. We've got to know what's behind us. It's only safe.'

The following day, as Sam helped Jason bolt the mirrors onto the ends of the foot bar, Nick and David came by to see what was taking shape in the little shed. They were a year above Jason and Sam at the village school but not so much older and superior that they couldn't offer a few words of encouragement and point out where improvements could be made.

'You're going to need some kind of brakes on that,' said David, as he stroked his peach fuzz chin in contemplation. 'Let me see…' And before long, he'd persuaded Jason that great speed was of no use when you couldn't stop. 'Why don't ya use the brake cable from an old bike? Or better yet, the wheelchair you got these wheels off will have a foot brake. You could fix that somehow and just give it a longer handle to grab down by the side, like this.' He mimicked lifting a lever down beside the seat, as though he was operating the handbrake on a car.

'While you're at it,' added Nick, puckering his mouth with distaste, ' you might wanna rethink that rope.'

Jason was all ears as Nick, gesturing like a flight attendant during a safety announcement, described a steering mechanism that would utilise a handle bar instead of an old piece of rope knotted through the ends of the foot bar.

'Just think, you could then fix lights to the handlebar so you can use it at night. How neat would that be? I've got a pair of old bike lights I don't need no more. You can have 'em if you promise to let me have a go.'

'That's a great idea!' exclaimed Jason, who was already thinking about a car battery and proper headlights.

Sam shook his head in resignation. This wasn't what he wanted at all. This was turning into a bloated grotesque buggy of sorts that would be of no use to anyone unless it had an engine. No, Sam liked the idea of keeping things simple.

But unfortunately for Sam, the kart that he had in mind, the one that could have been ready in no time at all was not the same kart that Jason and the others had begun to envision. It seemed that almost every day someone came up with a new suggestion to enhance The Beast as it had been christened and whether that suggestion came from Jason, or his brother Guy, or David or Nick it was usually given the thumbs up which then required another day of scrounging around for parts.

Sam's protests fell on deaf ears because in everything but the removable roof that was suggested so the kart could be used when it rained, he was outvoted. They did however, adapt the hood from a pram which could be removed when not needed, but Sam still viewed this as an unnecessary addition and a waste of time and effort. Armrests were added to the sides of the seat and mudguards for the rear wheels were fashioned from a sheet of corrugated tin and painted bright red to match the scrap of carpet that Jason finally found.

It was another week before The Beast was finally ready for its maiden run and as it was wheeled proudly out into the burning August sunshine, everyone thought it looked incredible. With its large wheels at the rear and small at the front they all thought it looked like a miniature dragster. Even Sam had to admit that it looked amazing.

Excitement gripped the little group as well as anticipation because they hadn't yet decided who was going to have first go.

'Well, there we go,' said Jason, wiping a quick rag over the shiny red slithers of tin that shrouded the rear wheels. 'The moment we been waiting for.'

The others each gave a word of two of appreciation for the completion of such a grand feat. Then there was a moment's silence as everyone stared at The Beast and then glanced expectantly at the faces of their friends.

'I reckon Sam should have first go,' said Jason. 'It was his idea, after all. Anyone think different?'

No one did. Indeed, an atmosphere of relief breezed through the group that the decision had been made without any squabbling.

'So, where shall we go with it?' asked Nick.

'Best place will be up behind the school, won't it?' said Sam. 'It's good and smooth and steep.'

'We'll have to watch out for cars,' said Nick.

'Yeah, but one of us can stay up the top and keep a look out and one of us at the bottom,' said Jason. 'That's no problem.'

'Or we could use the road that leads down to the tip,' offered David.

'It's nice and long,' said Sam.

'And twisty,' added David.

'But not as steep,' said Jason. 'And we wanna go as fast as we can.'

'There won't be so many cars there though,' said Nick.

The boys mulled over the choices for a few moments but then Jason seemed to make up the group's mind.

'I reckon up behind the school will be best.'

Twenty minutes later, Sam was sitting in the mini seat trembling with the thrill of the unknown. His bottom was just inches from the hot, unforgiving surface of the road which fell away from his eye line like the slope of a mountainside. Two hundred yards below, David, who had taken up position by the run-off at a curve, waved the all clear.

Jason was coiled like a spring behind the kart in readiness to offer the initial shove.

'Ready?' he asked, over Sam's shoulder. Sam nodded. His mouth was too dry to respond verbally.

'Okay. On yer marks…get set…GO!' Jason grunted as his soles pressed into the tarmac. The heavy kart surged forward and Sam's neck snapped back. The road reverberated through his feet and legs and through his grip on the handlebars as the wheels turned faster and faster. The tarmac began to sweep by beneath him and the edges of his vision blurred. The air rushed into his face and flew past his ears with a roar that drowned out everything except the yelps and shouts from the others. David was jumping up and down at the bottom as though his team had just scored the winning goal and he drew nearer by the second.

Sam felt as though he was going faster than he'd ever been on his bike, probably even faster than his dad would drive on the same stretch of road and as he approached the corner he pulled up the brake lever to reduce his speed and yelled out an ecstatic, 'Yaaaa-hooooooo!'

When he came to a stop his fringe was standing up in the shape of a fan. His heart was beating a hard and fast rhythm too and he couldn't wait to have another go.

David, who was clearly itching for his turn, ran over and congratulated him.

However, Sam had been right all along. The kart was far too heavy and cumbersome to drag or push up hill and virtually impossible for one of them to do so on their own. David had to help him that first time and when they were halfway up the hill, Jason came down to lend his muscle too. Having said that, the kart saw non-stop action for the first three days of its life, with all four boys taking turns and screaming hilariously from the mini seat. They took it to the road that led to the tip as well and enjoyed the longer, snakier but ultimately slower ride and they even tried it there after sunset when they could steer by the lights on the handlebars but this was less impressive than the idea promised. Then, after three days, they all got tired of dragging and pushing its weight around and so for the rest of the holidays it sat idle in the shed gathering cobwebs and dust.

At the End of the Day

I'm a stone's throw from home now and the shadows of a sunny day have long since lain down and turned to dusk. A clotted cream moon rises in the east as the humidity in the air continues to evaporate into a cool, clear sky bleeding away the temperature along with the light.

I hear Molly crying from several doors down the street and I quicken my step. It doesn't sound like the red-faced wail fuelled by temper or the irritating whine of protest that she sometimes uses to try to win her wars but a genuinely unhappy weep; a malaise on her poor young spirit. Wondering what's upset her so, I approach the front door.

It's happened before (to my shame) that upon returning from a bad day at the office and hearing little Molly hell bent on screaming the walls down, I've turned right around and gone and sat in the nearby pub for an hour or two. It's difficult to defend such an action, I know, but when one has suffered at work and is truly in desperate need of solace at the end of the day, it's hard to walk into such an ear-splitting atmosphere.

But tonight her obvious distress tugs firmly at my heartstrings and fills me with nothing more than a longing to comfort her. The difference, or at least the only one I can think of, is that today I have endured the most terrible working day of my life. There were times, particularly as the afternoon trudged on, when the only thing that stopped me throwing it all in was the thought of my baby girl and of the promise I made to her as I held her in my arms that very first time, a promise that I would provide for her to the very best of my ability. Throwing away a well-paid position in the city would be a gamble in anyone's book and could well lead to financial ruin but I have survived another day and I'm determined to persevere. Whether my resolve has a limit, I cannot say but it has been a day that I hope will never, ever be repeated.

Like a portent of disaster, it had started with the boiler going out during my morning shower and it just went downhill from there. That shockingly cold water needling my drowsy body had been like a slap in the face from a passing stranger and it had tempered my mood for the rest of the day. I simply couldn't shake off the feeling of irritation.

After that, I was living a comedy of errors and it was one thing after another. A shoelace broke, I couldn't find my pass card to get into the office, I got locked in the bathroom when the door handle broke off and my pen oozed a dark inky patch into the breast pocket of my shirt. All this before I'd even left home. Then I missed my bus to the station, which in turn made me miss my train, which in turn made me arrive at work nearly an hour late.

By this time there was a hammer clanging against an anvil inside my head. Unfortunately, a meeting with an important client had been scheduled early and well, being blamed for the likely loss of a fat contract saw me snapping at everyone all day, such was the misery that stewed within me.

The journey home had offered no relief either with cancellations and packed carriages full of irritated, odorous individuals. And on top of it all like the cherry on the cake, I narrowly missed being hit by a lorry as I dashed across the road from the station to catch the bus before it pulled away from the stop.

Gina sounds spent as she tries to calm our little lamb and as I step inside the house I sense from her tone that she's had a bad day as well. They are upstairs so I assume that she's still trying to put Molly to bed. On the plus side, at least I'll get to see my little darling before she goes to sleep.

I call out but there's no answer.

Oh! But it feels so good to be home, today more than ever. The sense of peace one gets from closing the front door on a demanding world can often feel like a shot of morphine in the arm.

The aroma of dinner wanders through from the kitchen teasing my taste buds and reminding my stomach of its emptiness and I can almost taste that glass of wine waiting to soothe my frayed nerves.

But before I do anything I want to see my girls. After such a testing day, they're the greatest comfort for a man. The rest doesn't come close. And I know that's something I don't keep in mind often enough.

Prickly voices from a soap opera spew out of the TV into an empty sitting room, which from where I'm standing at the foot of the stairs, looks as though it's witnessed the explosion of a toy box. Normally, the mess and the waste of electricity would have me muttering my displeasure but not tonight. Tonight I don't care. Such things are so trivial as to not be worth a thought.

Dear little Molly with her chubby little cheeks and her bright, trusting eyes. She's only been around a short time but she really is the centre of my life. She's shown me what it's all about and quite simply it's all about her. I can't wait to spend a few precious moments with her before she (hopefully) settles down and drifts away to some magical land of dreams. It doesn't matter that she's crying her eyes out - tonight I just want to be with her. I call out again as I take the stairs two at a time but her crying drowns out my voice.

Don't worry darling, Daddy's coming. I'll make you feel better. I call out again hoping that my voice will quieten her.

'Please Molly. For goodness sake, be quiet!' Poor Gina. She sounds absolutely frazzled. Don't worry darling, I'm coming. I'll make you feel better.

It's funny that my happiness to be home is overwhelming me this evening. It's almost as though I've been away for a fortnight or more, not just a single day and the nerves that were recently frayed and screaming out for some kind of relaxant now tingle with excitement. Of course, they've tingled with excitement before, many times, but most notably on my wedding day and on the day Molly was born. The thought says it all.

The crying gains volume as I get nearer to the source and when I reach the landing I call out again. The sweet, floral fragrance of bath time replaces the palate-arousing aroma downstairs as I move towards Molly's room and stand in the doorway. Gina is picking up dirty laundry from the floor. She rises and brushes loose strands of hair from her face and curls them behind her ears. She looks exhausted and yet at the same time beautiful and I feel an enormous swell of pride that our daughter has inherited her looks. Here they are then; the two most beautiful people in my world.

In the cot bed, Molly stands with her hands on the rail. Tears are streaming down her glistening red cheeks and her entire upper body shudders as she gasps for her next breath. My heart bleeds for her.

'Hey, sweetheart, what's all this crying about?' I step into the room hoping my tone will console her. Gina turns to me and her hands are full of little clothes and a soiled nappy. She steps towards me as I step towards her, my arms preparing to comfort her. And then she's behind me, on the landing heading into to bathroom, leaving me with a feeling I've not felt before.

I turn to follow her and the mirror on Molly's wall catches my eye. Something's missing from the reflection and it takes me a few seconds to realise what it is. Me.

I'm not there.

And then I understand.

I'm back there in an instant. Standing - although not really - in the road by the station among a small gathering of people. They're looking down at my limp and twisted body. My face no longer carries the tension of my day; I look as though I could be sleeping but in a really uncomfortable position. One of the onlookers is the driver of the lorry and I know this even though I've never seen him behind the wheel. He's mumbling incoherently about this and that and how it's not his fault. It's odd but I don't feel sad. Just disoriented.

And unsure what I should do.

But then it all becomes clear.

Also by M.K. Aston

Woeful and Roses

www.ingramcontent.com/pod-product-compliance
Lightning Source LLC
Chambersburg PA
CBHW020242130626
46549CB00005B/2024